be
strong &
curvaceous

be
strong &
curvaceous

an all about us novel

SHELLEY ADINA

Faith
Words

NEW YORK
BOSTON
NASHVILLE

Scripture quotations marked NIV are taken from the *Holy Bible, New International Version®*. NIV®. Copyright © 1973, 1978, 1984 by International Bible Society. Used by permission of Zondervan Publishing House. All rights reserved.

FaithWords

Hachette Book Group

237 Park Avenue

New York, NY 10017

Visit our Web site at www.faithwords.com.

FaithWords is a division of Hachette Book Group, Inc.

The FaithWords name and logo are trademarks of Hachette Book Group, Inc.

Printed in the United States of America

First Edition: January 2009

10 9 8 7 6 5 4 3 2 1

Library of Congress Cataloging-in-Publication Data

Adina, Shelley.
   Be strong & curvaceous / Shelley Adina. — 1st ed.
      p. cm.
   Summary: Carly, a Mexican American scholarship student at exclusive Spencer Academy in San Francisco, hides her status from her wealthy school friends until her new room-mate, a Scottish aristocrat, is threatened by an angry young man and needs Carly's—and God's—help.
   ISBN-13: 978-0-446-17799-3
   ISBN-10: 0-446-17799-7
   [1. Stalking—Fiction. 2. Social classes—Fiction. 3. Christian life—Fiction. 4. Dating (Social customs)—Fiction. 5. High schools—Fiction. 6. Schools—Fiction. 7. Mexican Americans—Fiction. 8. San Francisco (Calif.)—Fiction.] I. Title.
   PZ7.A261147Be 2009
   [Fic]—dc22

                                                                2008012626

For Cindy and Spencer

acknowledgments

This book was inspired by a true story. On January 29, 2001, eighteen-year-old Kelly Bennett alerted police to the contents of a packet of photographs she'd processed in her part-time job behind a drugstore photo counter. Because of her courage and quick thinking, Al deGuzman was arrested before he could detonate homemade bombs and commit mass murder at De Anza College in Cupertino, California—on the same day my husband was scheduled to be in class.

Thanks, Kelly.

be
strong &
curvaceous

"Be strong and courageous. Do not be afraid or terrified because of them, for the Lord your God goes with you; he will never leave you nor forsake you."

—*Deuteronomy 31:6 (NIV)*

chapter 1

BE CAREFUL WHAT you wish for.

I used to think that was the dumbest saying ever. I mean, when you wish for something, by definition it's wonderful, right? Like a new dress for a party. Or a roommate as cool as Gillian Chang or Lissa Mansfield. Or a guy noticing you after six months of being invisible. Before last term, of course I wanted those wishes to come true.

I should have been more careful.

Let me back up a little. My name is Carolina Isabella Aragon Velasquez . . . but that doesn't fit on school admission forms, so when I started first grade, it got shortened up to Carolina Aragon—Carly to my friends. Up until I was a sophomore, I lived with my mother and father, my older sister Alana and little brother Antony in a huge house in Monte Sereno, just south of Silicon Valley. Papa's company invented some kind of security software for stock exchanges, and he and everyone who worked for him got rich.

Then came Black Thursday and the stock market crash, and suddenly my mom was leaving him and going to live with her parents in Veracruz, Mexico, to be an artist and find herself. Alana finished college and moved to Austin, Texas, where we have lots of relatives. Antony, Papa, and I moved to a condo about the size of our old living room, and since Papa spends so much time on the road, where I've found myself since September is boarding school.

The spring term started in April, and as I got out of the limo Papa sends me back to Spencer Academy in every Sunday night—even though I'm perfectly capable of taking the train—I couldn't help but feel a little bubble of optimism deep inside. Call me corny, but the news that Vanessa Talbot and Brett Loyola had broken up just before spring break had made the last ten days the happiest I'd had since my parents split up. Even flying to Veracruz, courtesy of Papa's frequent-flyer miles, and being introduced to my mother's boyfriend hadn't put a dent in it.

Ugh. Okay, I lied. *So* not going there.

Thinking about Brett now. Dark, romantic eyes. Curly dark hair, cut short because he's the captain of the rowing team. Broad shoulders. Fabulous clothes he wears as if he doesn't care where he got them.

Oh, yeah. Much better.

Lost in happy plans for how I'd finally get his attention (I was signing up to be a chem tutor first thing because, let's face it, he needs me), I pushed open the door to my room and staggered in with my duffel bags.

My hands loosened and I dropped everything with a thud.

There were Vuitton suitcases all over the room. Enough for an entire *family*. In fact, the trunk was so big you could put a family *in* it—the kids, at least.

"Close the door, why don't you?" said a bored British voice, with a barely noticeable roll on the *r*. A girl stepped out from behind the wardrobe door.

Red hair in an explosion of curls.

Fishnet stockings to *here* and glossy Louboutin ankle boots.

Blue eyes that grabbed you and made you wonder why she was so . . . not interested in whether you took another breath.

Ever.

How come no one had told me I was getting a roommate? And who could have prepared me for this, anyway?

"Who are you?"

"Mac," she said, returning to the depths of the wardrobe. Most people would have said, "What's your name?" back. She didn't.

"I'm Carly." Did I feel lame or what?

She looked around the door. "Pleasure. Looks like we're to be roommates." Then she went back to hanging things up.

There was no point in restating the obvious. I gathered my scattered brains and tried to remember what a good hostess was supposed to do. "Did someone show you where the dining room is? Supper is between five and six-thirty, and I usually—"

"Carrie. I expected my own room," she said, as if I hadn't been talking. "Whom do I speak to?"

"It's *Carly*. And Ms. Tobin's the dorm mistress for this floor."

"Fine. What were you saying about tea?"

I took a breath and remembered that one of us was what my brother calls *couth*. As opposed to *un*. "You're welcome to come with me and my friends if you want."

Pop! went the latches on the trunk. She threw up the lid and looked at me over the top of it, her reddish eyebrows lifting in amusement.

"Thanks so much. But I'll pass."

Okay, even I have my limits. I picked up my duffel, dropped it on the end of my bed, and left her to it. Maybe by the time I got back from tea—er, supper—she'd have convinced Ms. Tobin to give her a room in another dorm.

The way things looked, this *chica* would probably demand the headmistress's suite.

"WHAT A *MO guai nuer*," Gillian said over her tortellini and asparagus. "I can't believe she snubbed you like that."

"You of all people," Lissa agreed, "who wouldn't hurt someone's feelings for anything."

"I wanted to—if I could have come up with something scathing." Lissa looked surprised, as if I'd shocked her. Well, I may not put my feelings out there for everyone to see, like Gillian does, but I'm still entitled to have them. "But you know how you freeze when you realize you've just been cut off at the knees?"

"What happened to your knees?" Jeremy Clay put his plate of linguine down and slid in next to Gillian. They traded a smile that made me feel sort of hollow inside—not the way I'd felt after Mac's little setdown, but . . . like I was missing out on something. Like they had a secret and weren't telling.

You know what? Feeling sorry for yourself is not the way to start off a term. I smiled at Jeremy. "Nothing. How was your break? Did you get up to New York the way you guys had planned?"

He glanced at Gillian. "Yeah, I did."

Argh. Men. Never ask them a yes/no question. "And? Did you have fun? Shani said she had a blast after the initial shock."

Gillian grinned at me. "That's a nice way of saying that my grandmother scared the stilettos off her. At first. But then Nai-Nai realized Shani could eat anyone under the table, even my brothers, no matter what she put in front of her, so after that they were best friends."

"My grandmother's like that, too," I said, nodding in sympathy. "She thinks I'm too thin, so she's always making pots of *mole* and stuff. Little does she know."

It's a fact that I have way too much junk in my trunk. Part of the reason my focus is in history, with as many fashion design electives as I can get away with, is that when I make my own clothes, I can drape and cut to accentuate the positive and make people forget that big old negative following me around.

"You aren't too thin or too fat." Lissa is a perfect four. She's also the most loyal friend in the world. "You're just right. If I had your curves, I'd be a happy woman."

Time to change the subject. The last thing I wanted to do was talk about my body in front of a guy, even if he belonged to someone else. "So, did you guys get to see *Pride and Prejudice—The Musical*? Shani said you were bribing someone to get tickets."

"Close," Gillian said. "My mom is on the orchestra's board, so we got seats in the first circle. You'd have loved it. Costume heaven."

"I would have." I sighed. "Why did I have to go to Veracruz for spring break? How come I couldn't have gone to New York, too?"

I hoped I sounded rhetorical. The truth was, there wasn't any money for trips to New York to see the hottest musical on Broadway with my friends. Or for the clothes to wear once I got there—unless I made them myself.

"That's it, then." Gillian waved a grape tomato on the end of her fork. "Next break, you and Lissa are coming to see me. Not in the summer—no one in their right mind stays in the city in July. But at Christmas."

"Maybe we'll go to Veracruz," Lissa suggested. "Or you guys can come to Santa Barbara and I'll teach you to surf."

"That sounds perfect," I said. Either of Lissa's options wouldn't cost very much. New York, on the other hand, would. "I like warm places for my winter holidays."

"Good point," Gillian conceded. "So do I."

"Notice how getting through the last term of junior year isn't even on your radar?" Jeremy asked no one in particular. "It's all about vacations with you guys."

"Vacations are our reward," Gillian informed him. "You have to have something to get you through finals."

"Right, like you have to worry," he scoffed, bumping shoulders with her in a chummy way.

"She does," Lissa said. "She has to get *me* through finals."

While everyone laughed, I got up and walked over to the dessert bar. *Crème brulée*, berry parfaits, and German chocolate cake. You know you're depressed when even Dining Services' *crème brulée*—which puts a dreamy look in the eyes of just about everyone who goes here—doesn't get you excited.

I had to snap out of it. Thinking about all the things I didn't have and all the things I couldn't do would get me precisely nowhere. I had to focus on the good things.

My friends.

How lucky I was to have won the scholarship that got me into Spencer.

And how much luckier I was that in two terms, no one had figured out I was a scholarship kid. Okay, so Gillian is a scholarship kid, too, but her dad is the president of a multinational bank. She thinks it's funny that he made her practice the piano so hard all those years, and that's what finally got her away from him. Who is my father? No one. Just a hardworking guy. He was so proud of me when that acceptance letter came that I didn't have the heart to tell him there was more to succeeding here than filling a minority quota and getting good grades.

Stop it. Just because you can't flit off to New York to catch a show or order up the latest designs from Fashion Week doesn't mean your life is trash. Get ahold of your sense of proportion.

I took a berry parfait—blueberries have lots of antioxidants—and turned back to the table just as the dining room doors opened. They seemed to pause in their arc, giving my new roommate plenty of time to stroll through before they practically genuflected closed behind her. She'd changed out of the fishnets into heels and a black sweater tossed over a simple leaf-green dress that absolutely screamed Paris—Rue Cambon, to be exact. Number 31, to be even more exact. Chanel Couture.

My knees nearly buckled with envy.

"Is *that* Carly's roommate?" I heard Lissa ask.

Mac seemed completely unaware that everyone in the dining room was watching her as she floated across the floor like a runway model, collected a plate of Portobello mushroom ravioli and salad, and sat at the empty table next to the big window that faced out onto the quad.

Lissa was still gazing at her, puzzled. "I know I've seen her before."

I hardly heard her.

Because not only had the redhead cut into line ahead of Vanessa Talbot, Dani Lavigne, and Emily Overton, she'd also invaded their prime real estate. No one sat at that table unless they'd sacrificed a freshman at midnight, or whatever it was that people had to do to be friends with them.

When Vanessa turned with her plate, I swear I could hear the collective intake of breath as her gaze locked on the stunning interloper sitting with her back to the window, calmly cutting her ravioli with the edge of her fork.

"Uh oh," Gillian murmured. "Let the games begin."

chapter 2

VANESSA, DANI, AND EMILY formed a fighting V and strolled to the table with their plates.

"Excuse me, do we know you?" Dani asked politely.

"Poor thing," Mac said. "I'm so sorry about the short-term memory loss. No, we haven't met."

Dani's mouth worked while she tried to figure out whether or not she'd just been insulted.

Vanessa stepped in front of her. "My name is Vanessa Talbot."

"Pleasure. Mac."

"Mac?" Emily repeated. "What kind of a name is that?"

Vanessa ignored her. "And you're sitting in my seat."

Mac looked at the empty table, which could seat eight. "Really?"

"Really. I suggest you move. My friends and I sit here. Everyone knows that except clueless noobs."

Mac's face dimpled with laughter, as if Vanessa had told her a real knee-slapper. "I'd say you were the clueless one, if you think *that's* any reason to move. Sit where you like, darling. Do enjoy the ravioli. It's marvelous." And she went back to her pasta.

Vanessa's face set into a porcelain mask. "This is the last time I'll ask you nicely. After that . . ."

Mac glanced at her. "What? You'll turn me into a ferret?"

Even from where I stood, I could see the color burn its way into Vanessa's cheeks. When was the last time anyone had stood up to her? Certainly not this year. Well, except for Gillian and Lissa, first term.

"You wish," Vanessa said. "Try a social outcast."

"From your society?" Mac drawled. "What a terrible loss."

"Do you have any idea who she is?" Dani hissed. "You big, redheaded loser."

"Vanessa Talbot. Hmm." Mac consulted an imaginary PDA in her head. "Daughter of a former U.N. Secretary and Eurotrash." She rolled her eyes. "Such a bore."

"At least you've done your research," Vanessa snapped. "Unfortunately, you don't seem to be anyone."

"No one you'd know, and I'd prefer to keep it that way." Mac looked the three of them over. "Are you staying or going?"

I tried to keep my grin under control as a ripple of something that was almost laughter sighed through the room. This was the best thing that had happened since the infamous food fight last term, but nobody dared to laugh outright. The truth was, Vanessa was stuck. If she stalked off to another table, she and her posse would lose their territory. If she didn't, she'd have to let Mac sit with them—and that might imply she'd accepted her.

Can you say *lose/lose*?

Mac smiled—not a victorious or malicious smile, but the sweet kind. Like frosting that comes in a can—close enough to fool you into thinking it's the real thing. With a huff of impatience, as though she didn't have any more time to waste on Mac while her food got cold, Vanessa slid into a seat.

I finally got my feet moving and took my blueberries back to our table, where Gillian and Lissa telegraphed "Did you see that?" and "What's going to happen now?" to me with their eyes.

It didn't take long for us to find out. Vanessa was not the kind of girl who let anything go unresolved—especially a power struggle. I'd only been here a week or two when I'd learned that. She was so used to winning that it never occurred to her there could be any other outcome.

She made a show of picking at her lunch, then reached for her drink. Dani said something to her, and, whoops! Her soda went flying . . . all over Mac's lime-green Chanel dress.

I would have screamed and burst into tears. Mac stood slowly, looking down at her lap, where a brown stain spread. Coke dripped slowly from the hem to the floor.

"Oh, I'm so sorry," Vanessa said, while Dani made *tsk*ing noises and Emily offered a handful of napkins. "I hope it's washable."

Every female in the room knew it wasn't. Every one of us knew Vanessa had just done the equivalent of painting a mustache on the *Mona Lisa*.

"Eurotrash." Mac finally sighed. Lifting her head, she gave it a slow, regretful shake. "What a pity a person can't overcome her DNA."

And she floated out of the room as effortlessly as she'd come in, leaving Vanessa fuming behind her.

Vanessa, 1. Mac, 2.

I wondered when Round Two would begin—and what kind of fallout there would be. At the moment I couldn't see any positives about being Mac's roommate.

None at all.

AFTER DINNER, Lissa and Gillian came back to my room to talk over the excitement.

"It's like the Slayer," Lissa said. "In every generation there can be only one, you know?"

"You are such a dork. What'd you do, watch all your *Buffy* DVDs over break?" Gillian flopped down on my bed. "But you're right. I can't see this going on for very long. One of them is going to kill the other, or get her expelled by the end of the week. And it's only Tuesday." She blinked. "Is all this stuff hers?"

"Yep." I sank into my desk chair, leaving the other end of my bed for Lissa. "I left all my Vuittons at home." Not.

"Wow. And I thought I had a lot of stuff."

"I just don't know where she—"

The door opened and Mac stepped in. "Company?" she inquired pleasantly. "Lovely."

Turning her back on us, she shrugged off the black sweater and unzipped the dress, tossing it in a corner. She kicked off her shoes and pulled on a pair of jeans and a T-shirt.

"Will—will you be able to do something about the dress?" I asked, hoping I sounded concerned. There was no hope of being friends, of course, but a catastrophe like this deserved some mourning over the body, at least.

She glanced at it. "Oh, I don't know. Haven't the faintest idea where to get it seen to. I'll probably just order another one."

From Chanel Couture. In Paris. *Sure, I'll take two.*

"It's still a shame. Vanessa is such a—" Gillian stopped herself, then crossed the carpet and held out a hand. "I'm Gillian Chang. Carly says you're called Mac. Is that short for something?"

Mac ran a glance over her—tennies, jeans, cashmere sweater, face—and shook hands. "Hello. It's short for MacPhail."

Lissa got up, too. "I'm Lissa Mansfield. It's a pleasure to meet anyone with the spine to stand up to Vanessa. What's your first name?"

She got the same once-over before Mac spoke. "I prefer Mac."

O-o-kay. I took a tiny bit of comfort from the fact that she was an equal-opportunity snubber.

But unlike me, Lissa didn't go away quietly. "You know, I could swear we've met before. Your face is familiar, for some reason."

"I don't see how." Mac picked up a brush and ran it through her unruly curls. "I've never been to California in my life."

"What about New York? Montreal? Vancouver?"

Mac shook her head, twisting her hair up and securing it with a clip.

"MacPhail. Are you from the U.K.? Scotland?"

"Originally. I go to school in London, of course. We have to do one term of cultural exchange. That's how I ended up here." She made it sound like she was researching pygmies in Borneo—against her will.

"What was your first choice?" I meant it as a joke, but she didn't take it that way.

"New Zealand."

Oh. Never mind. Was it possible to have thirty seconds of conversation with this girl without being flattened?

"Well, I'm glad you came here," Gillian said. "Vanessa could use a little humility."

"Oh? What have you got against her?"

Whoa. Was she switching sides? Did money and European connections stick together, no matter what?

"Me? Nothing. Except that she tried to steal my boyfriend last term. And she set Lissa up—"

"I don't think Mac would be very interested in that," Lissa interrupted. "Come on, Gillian. Carly, are you coming to prayer circle? It's Tuesday."

"Absolutely. Just let me change my blouse. I got pesto on this one."

Mac looked from them, waiting by the door, to me, tearing off the babydoll top I had on and reaching for a tailored blouse that made my waist look half an inch smaller. "Prayer circle?" she said, in the same tone some people would say, "Head lice?"

"Sure." Gillian smiled at her. "Tuesday nights, seven o'clock. Everyone's welcome."

"Term always starts on a Wednesday," Lissa put in. "It kicks it off on a good note, I think."

"Is that a Christian thing?" Mac asked.

Lissa nodded. I finished buttoning up the blouse and gave it a final tug. *Jump right in.* "Want to come?"

Mac actually shuddered. "I'm going out. Where do you lot party 'round here?"

We exchanged a look. "You'd have to ask someone like Vanessa about that. She probably knows where the underage clubs are."

"The what?"

"Underage clubs," I repeated. "You're sixteen, right?"

"Do you seriously think I'd waste my time with children?"

"Let me rephrase. You'd have to ask Vanessa about that. She probably knows where you can get a fake I.D."

"What has that got to do with clubbing? Do you know or not?"

I gave up. "I don't. Sorry." I grabbed Lissa and Carly by the arms and hustled them out the door. "Have fun."

We were halfway to Room 216 before anyone spoke. "I know what I'm praying about tonight," Lissa said.

"No kidding." My voice sounded grim, even to me. "And while you're at it, pray that Tobin finds her another room."

GILLIAN HADN'T HAD TIME to put up her usual neon-colored prayer-circle posters, so I didn't expect many people to show. Which, as it turned out, was a good thing. Because ever since I started school here and started hanging around with her and Lissa, it had slowly sunk in that they were different. I mean, I try to be as nice as possible to everyone. I'd rather make a friend than an enemy, you know? Especially at Spencer, where friendships seem to extend to college and beyond, creating this network of alumni that are all wealthy, famous, and connected.

But like I said, there was something . . . more . . . about Gillian and Lissa. Something that I wanted to be a part of with them, even though it scared me. I'd tried to talk with Shani about it last term, but she just got weirded out and changed the subject. So while I'd been in Mexico, I'd had plenty of time on my own to think. To locate the family Bible in my *abuelita*'s room and dip into it. To realize that, since September, I'd been circling around a choice and I couldn't see yet what lay beyond it.

And now here we were, heading for the very first prayer circle of the term, where something told me I was going to stop circling and start facing that choice head-on.

Room 216, as usual, had gotten filled up with junk over the break. If everyone goes away, where does the stuff come from? It's a mystery. Anyway, we spent about ten minutes locating the chairs and piling cardboard boxes out in the hall for the maintenance staff to take away. The unofficial art exhibit had gone from odd sculptures and oils to a collection of graphic art mounted on foam core and tacked up along the wall, above the Edwardian wainscoting.

One of the pictures caught my eye. A lithe female figure was caught in mid-kick, taking out an evil-looking cloud with yellow eyes. Lettered neatly in the bottom left corner was a name: *G. Chang.*

"Gillian, is this yours?"

My loudmouth friend, who has never backed down from anything, that I know of—well, except during that whole episode with Lucas Hayes last term—actually blushed. "I told them not to put that in here," she mumbled. "It's not very good."

"I think it's really good. I didn't even know you could draw. That graphic arts class must really kick." I glanced at the panel again. "No pun intended."

"Kaz thinks it's good," Lissa put in, moving the chairs into a tight circle. "And he should know. Some New York editor asked for his whole book during break."

"Wow." I didn't know a thing about graphic novels or publishing, but this sounded pretty impressive to me. "Did you guys see a lot of each other when you were down there?"

Lissa nodded and sat, stretching her long legs out and crossing her ankles. "Sure. He's my best friend."

Personally, I had my own ideas about that. I'd seen the expression on Kaz's face that night at the Benefactors' Day Ball, when he'd saved Lissa on the dance floor. I don't have the biggest pile of ex-files in the world, but even I can tell when a guy is *apasionado* for a girl. But probably if I said anything, she'd get all uneasy about it, and it would mess up what they had going.

Better to mind my own business.

And what was I doing thinking about art and boys, anyway, when I was supposed to be thinking about prayer circle?

I sat next to Lissa just as the door opened and Shani Hanna came in, with Jeremy right behind her.

"Hey!" Gillian grabbed her in a hug, and hugged Jeremy, too, for good measure. Not that I noticed him complaining. "Did you just get here?"

"Yeah. There was so much traffic coming north from the airport that I thought I'd miss it. How are you guys?" Shani hugged each of us in turn. Today her hair was french-braided in a circle like a crown around her head. It suited her perfectly.

"Great, now that you're here." I grinned at her. "Are you sure you don't keep a personal stylist in your closet?"

"No kidding," Lissa said. "No human female can be this good

with her own hair. You have a different 'do every time I look at you."

"Ease up," Shani said, pretending to hide behind her hands. "I told Gillian when I was at her place. I spent, like, thousands of hours on my own when I was a kid. The housemaids used to hang out with me, and we had this mini-salon going in my bedroom. We'd spend hours learning how to do hair and makeup and reading *Essence* and *Cosmo* by the inch."

I thought of the way our place had been when I was a kid. Noisy, flamboyant, with relatives coming and going all the time. My dad had bought his parents a house down the street from us with his first million, and their place was the same as ours. No relative was allowed to come through the San Jose airport without at least staying overnight. And since my grandparents each had half a dozen siblings, that made for a lot of houseguests.

Now we're down to three bedrooms and two baths in the condo, and my grandparents are gone and the houses sold. Even so, when Dad is in town, we have a lot of company. Poor Shani. From what she'd told me, growing up in that big mansion in Chicago must have been like growing up in a walk-in freezer. She did pretty well for being brought up by housemaids moonlighting as nannies, if you ask me. On top of a great sense of style and genius with her hair, she's sassy, smart, and has a comeback for everything.

She and Gillian are just the way I'd like to be. Fearless.

Again with the monkey brain. I needed to settle my thoughts. What was wrong with me? It was like my mind was doing total God avoidance. Not that I was really trying to avoid Him. But you know how it is with big decisions. You put them off until they either go away, solve themselves . . . or become Really Big Issues. I seemed to have arrived at door number three while I was aiming at doors one and two. Which happens a lot with me.

"It's seven, you guys," Gillian said. "Let's get started. I guess we don't have to do intros this time, do we?"

We joined hands and Gillian started us off. As she prayed, I felt myself squeezing Lissa's and Jeremy's hands tighter and tighter. Shani passed. After her came Jeremy. I only had a few minutes to make up my mind—to walk up to that choice and face it head-on. To say yes—or no.

Poor Jeremy. As he finished praying, he gently tried to take his hand out of mine. I'd squeezed so hard it had turned red.

I closed my eyes and opened my mouth. Nothing came out.

Ten seconds went by. I tried again. Nada.

"Carly?" Gillian asked softly. "Are you okay?"

"I don't know," I managed. "Just give me a minute."

They did. Lissa's hand squeezed mine with reassurance. "Father," her voice came strong and sure, "please reach out and put Your hands around Carly. She needs You."

And suddenly I knew that was the answer. As simple as that— I needed God. And He, for some reason, needed me, too. And wasn't that the coolest thing?

"Father," I said, my voice getting stronger with every word, "thank You for wanting me. Thank You for my friends, who show me every day that needing You is a good thing. I want that, too." Happiness began to warm me, deep inside. "I want to be Your child for good."

And you know what?

It wasn't such a hard choice to make, after all.

EOverton	Major news flash!
VTalbot	If it's one more thing about that Brit I'm not interested.
EOverton	OK.
VTalbot	Well?
EOverton	But you said—
VTalbot	E, just spit it out.

EOverton   You know Lainey who helps in the admin office?

VTalbot   Chunky, bad cut, mom on the SFMOMA board?

EOverton   She's not that chunky.

VTalbot   The point, E.

EOverton   She just filed Mac's paperwork and you're not going to believe this.

VTalbot   She was expelled from West Heath. Big deal. So was my mom.

EOverton   Bigger than that. But the right country.

VTalbot   I don't have time for 20 Questions. I'm going over to Callum's.

EOverton   I found out her real name.

VTalbot   Don't tell me. She's Kathy Hilton's secret daughter.

EOverton   No. She's the Earl of Strathcairn's daughter. Full name Lady Lindsay Margaret Eithne MacPhail.

VTalbot   Lady???

EOverton   Who would call herself a stupid name like Mac when she's got a title?

VTalbot   Why should you care? You want to be friends now?

EOverton   Not until she apologizes to you.

VTalbot   Glad we got that settled. I'm off.

EOverton   Have fun.

VTalbot   I always do.

chapter 3

FTER PRAYER CIRCLE, we usually walked down the hill to graze in one of the restaurants on Fillmore, or just went to Starbucks for a latte. But tonight I was still in recovery. All I wanted to do was hang out and talk about what I'd decided with my friends. So everyone except Jeremy, who wasn't allowed in the girls' dorm, came back to my room with me.

"Oh, good." Gillian took in the empty room with a glance, and made herself at home on my bed. "We have the place to ourselves."

Nothing wrong with being glad about that, was there? I tried to imagine talking about choosing God with Mac in the room, lying negligently on her bed with a cynical, maybe even mocking, expression in her eyes. Nuh-uh. Impossible.

"I'm so happy." Lissa hugged me—for at least the fifth time between Room 216 and here—and flopped at Gillian's feet. "Now I feel like I can talk with you about anything."

I rummaged in the cupboard and found a jumbo bag of Ruffles. "You couldn't before?"

"Mostly. But not about everything. Now I feel . . . free."

I paused for a second, testing my emotions. "Know what? So do I. Isn't that weird?"

"Define *weird*," Shani said. "Weird was watching your face back there. Are you okay?"

"Yeah," I said softly. "More than okay. I feel peaceful. Like I finally did what God wanted and He's massively happy about it."

"But what did you do, exactly?" Shani's forehead was creased, like she was trying hard to solve a math problem from the senior textbook without having gone over the material first.

"I realized that needing Him was okay." How simple was that? How simple, and how amazingly complicated. "I've been dealing with this for months. As you guys could probably tell." How to put it so they'd understand? "And it got to the point where I had to do something. Or nothing. But I had to make up my mind. It almost felt like it had to happen now."

"Okay, that's weird," Shani said a little flatly. "Is God going to push you in front of a Muni bus, or what?"

"I saw it in a vision," I said solemnly. "Tomorrow, while I'm crossing to go to the field house."

Her face went slack, and I burst out laughing. "Come on, Shani. You know God doesn't do stuff like that."

Embarrassment mixed with a little defiance in her expression. "How would I know? You guys all seem to be the experts."

"Far from it," Lissa said with a snort. "Just ask Gillian about the first time I met her."

"She thought I was going to whip out the incense and smoke her out." Gillian grinned at her. "And I thought she was going to whip out the Humboldt County leaf and smoke *me* out."

I had to laugh. Talk about a collision in your expectations. "And you both turned out to be believers."

"Yeah, putting our absolute worst feet forward," Gillian said. "It's not about being perfect or experts. It's about listening and talking and having a relationship with a God who loves you more than anything."

"I wish I could believe that," Shani said, a little wistfully. "But I just can't wrap my brain around it."

"It's not the brain," I said quietly. "It's the heart. I felt like mine was going to explode. And not in a cardiac-arrest way." I waggled my hands, trying to gather up the right words. "A love way."

"Huh." Shani tried to take this in, then shook her head and got up. "I'm going to go up and finish unpacking," she said in a not-very-subtle change of subject. "Last term of junior year already. Everybody got their community service credits in?"

"Lots of stuff going on. I'm being a grunt on the prom committee—excuse me, the *Cotillion* committee." Trust Lissa to snag that one. And trust her to let Shani think she was getting away with avoiding the issue. "The seniors are in charge, so it's one of the few things Vanessa isn't running. Cotillion sounds so old-fashioned, doesn't it?"

"This is an old-fashioned kind of place," Gillian said. "Just don't make me wear a white gown and pretend to be a deb."

"I don't think debs exist in California," Lissa said. "The species went extinct in the fifties. Anyway, Vanessa's got her hooks in the really cool thing—the fashion show in June."

"Fashion show?" I might be a brand-new Christian, but that didn't mean other stuff couldn't get my attention. Especially if it had anything to do with clothes. "What kind of fashion show?"

"Charity gig, of course, meaning gobs of credits," Lissa said. "Word is it's going to be called Design Your Dreams. A bunch of San Francisco and L.A. designers are going to send their clothes and Spencer students will model them. The charity part is what the people will shell out for tickets. Students can model their own stuff, too, if they want. It's almost like an audition for the people who want to go into the fashion industry. *Project Runway* lite."

"And we haven't heard about this why?" I demanded. I would get a dress into that show or die. Period.

"Uh, because school hasn't officially started yet?" Shani pointed out. "Relax, girlfriend. You'll get your chance to strut your stuff in front of Stella McCartney."

"Or the Mulleavys," I said dreamily. "Or Tori Wu or—"

The door opened, and all of us turned to look. A little sinking hole formed in my stomach, draining the excitement and warmth out of the evening.

Mac looked us over. "Hello again."

"Mac, this is Shani. Shani, Mac." They nodded at each other.

"Did you have a nice time at tent meeting?" Mac shoved her trunk against the end of her bed and began pulling things out of it. A pair of riding boots and a helmet. Books. A leather jacket in black and red that looked as if it might be worn by a motorcycle racer. Shoes: heels, flats, sandals.

Lissa lost the thread of the most interesting conversation I'd had in weeks and watched the shoes come out of the trunk the way my grandma's chickens watch her hands when she brings the leftovers from dinner out into the yard.

"Not a tent meeting," I said. "Prayer circle. And yes, we did."

"Carly's a Christian now," Gillian told her. My hands jerked, as if they wanted to fly up and cover her mouth. "It was amazing. We were all just talking about it."

"You mean you weren't before?" Mac asked me. "After tea?"

"I—I'm not sure," I stammered. Could I feel any more uncomfortable? And why? I should be singing it from the school roof, shouldn't I?

"So what am I to expect now?" she went on. "You're not going to be a bore and preach or anything, are you? I really can't have that."

"No," I said. No fear of that. Or of speaking. Or of doing anything but ignoring each other.

"Good. What *are* you staring at?" she demanded of Lissa.

"Are those custom Balenciagas?" Lissa breathed, her gaze locked on the high-heeled sandals dangling from Mac's fingers.

"These?" She glanced at them. "I suppose they are. Good eye."

"My mother has a pair," Lissa said with longing.

"You can borrow them, if you like."

Lissa looked as though she'd died and gone to heaven. "Serious?"

Mac shrugged. "They're from the spring collection. When I get the fall ones, I won't want them anymore."

Which sort of put a different spin on it. She'd be better off donating them to Career Closet. Lissa straightened. "Thanks, but we're probably not the same size."

"Whatever." She lifted an eyebrow at me. "I found your Ms. Tobin. About the room arrangements."

"Oh?" *Please, Lord. Let her have found another room.*

"The only other empty bed, apparently, is with you." She glanced at Shani. "So since I'm already here, I may as well make the best of it."

"Could you be any more unkind?" Gillian inquired. Her tone might have been polite, but her eyes sure weren't. "Carly is the nicest person you could hope to meet. You don't need to treat her like trash. Or the rest of us, for that matter."

Mac smiled. "I have the cleaning staff deal with trash. I thought I was treating you rather differently."

Gillian was up off the bed by now. "Different is right. I suggest an attitude adjustment."

"I suggest you toddle off to bed, little rice ball."

Gillian flew into her face. "You want to repeat that?"

The smile had spread into a grin. Mac was enjoying this—

deliberately antagonizing anyone within reach. "Are you deaf, too? I said—"

"You didn't answer my question."

"Which one?"

"Why are you so mean?"

Mac shrugged. "What difference does it make? You can always leave."

"And Carly gets to be stuck here with you? We're better friends than that."

"Oh, are we all going to have a nice, cozy pajama party? Because if not, you're going to have to get out sooner rather than later. Do us a favor and make it sooner, would you?"

"Are you *looking* to make enemies?" Shani asked her. "Because let me tell you, this school isn't the place to do that, if you can help it."

"Why is it so different from anywhere else?" The emotional temperature in the room was this close to redlining, and she looked as cool and amused as if she were at a garden party.

"The people who go here make things happen," Shani said. "If you make enemies out of everybody, what's going to happen when you leave and want an internship or a summer job?"

"I'll blow dust in their faces, hopefully," she replied. "You can't possibly imagine that the opinions of anyone here matter to me."

Shani looked at me. "I'm so sorry, Carly, but I have to go. I can't take any more of this."

"Me, too," Gillian said. "Come on, Lissa."

As Lissa hugged me, she whispered, "The first thing the devil does is make you sorry you chose God. Don't let Mac get to you."

Easier said than done, I thought as I watched the door close behind them. I looked at the calendar on my desk.

Thirty, sixty . . . only seventy-three days left to go.

LISSA GRABBED ME the next day on our way to U.S. History. "Did you hear?"

"Hear what?"

Kids wove and split around us in the entry hall as Lissa dragged me off to the side under a big oil painting of Eleanor Spencer, the Countess of Carrick, who had founded the school when Edward VII was Prince of Wales. I'd never heard of her before I came here, but the gown she'd worn for her portrait had been designed by Worth in 1885, and I never missed an opportunity to study it on my way past.

"The big news about your roommate. And why she looked so familiar."

"Let me guess. She was on WhoWhatWearDaily-dot-com."

"No. Not recently, anyway."

"She was on some reality show."

"No."

"Gillian's cousin found her record in NCIC and you recognized her mug shot."

"No. Would you be serious?"

"I give up, then." I leaned in a little closer. "Personally, the only news I care about is that she's on the next British Airways flight to Heathrow."

"Sorry." Lissa made a rueful mouth. "Remember at Christmas I went to Scotland with my dad?"

"Uh-huh." He'd been approving locations for *The Middle Window*, his big Scottish historical that was opening in the fall. Penny Rose was doing the costumes, and that meant I knew as much about it as Lissa did—or maybe more. It also meant costuming loops springing up like mushrooms, a surge in eighteenth-century patterns being posted on the Web, people scouting out the garment districts in London and L.A., duplicating period fabrics. In other words, bliss. "You are totally taking us to the premiere. You know that."

"Of course. Focus, Carly. Remember when I said we went to this castle and the earl gave us tea and his horrible daughter went off on her horse so she wouldn't have to meet us?"

I stared at her as I connected the dots. "Tell me you're joking."

"Sadly, no. That's why she looked so familiar. Her school pictures were on the table and I was looking at them while Dad talked business with the earl."

Castle. Earl. "Someone should tell her she isn't royalty."

Lissa shook her head. "No kidding. But she's definitely the Lady Lindsay who blew Dad and me off. I wonder if she expects us to curtsy."

I shuddered. "How did I get so lucky? The only thing worse than having a horrible roommate is having a horrible roommate who's an aristocrat."

No wonder she'd been so blasé about the custom-designed Balenciaga shoes. Daddy was an earl. She probably went to all the Paris shows and designers begged her to wear their clothes, just for the publicity. And here I was, two generations away from prune pickers in the California fields—some of which I knew for a fact had been owned by Brett Loyola's family. The only reason I was even here was because I'd checked "Mexican American" on my application form and had landed a full ride for board and tuition. It wasn't often Spencer got to brag about its diversity.

Not that I'm bitter about it. I'm a realist. I help them with their quota requirements, and they help me get into an A-list college. Fair enough, right?

In U.S. History, the instructor talked about the suffragettes tying themselves to the railings in front of the White House. I gazed at her and didn't see any of it—instead, I saw the shoes and the expensive leathers coming out of Mac's—sorry, Lady Lindsay's—trunk.

It had been easy enough to fool people into thinking my family was as well off as any student's here. After all, Papa sent a limo for me every Friday night to take me down to San Jose. What they didn't know was it was the company limo, and the driver was my cousin Enrique, who made a few bucks on the side by doing it.

How was I going to keep my secret, with Mac's sardonic blue gaze taking in every outfit, every shoe, every clever knockoff handbag? What if she decided to talk about the sad state of my closet? What if it got back to Vanessa Talbot, and therefore to Brett?

I was invisible to him now, but at least there was hope that he'd notice me. I mean, as it was, once in a while he nodded to me when I handed him things in the chem lab. But if I was just the Mexican scholarship case, I wouldn't have a prayer. The doors of friendship—or anything else—would slam shut, and there I'd be, permanently outside in the cold.

There would probably be a dance or reception connected to Design Your Dreams, and Brett would find some lovely trust fund baby in a couture dress to parade on his arm. I didn't have a trust fund, but I wanted to be that girl on his arm, wearing the dress that had won major attention at the fashion show. That had maybe even landed me a summer internship with a designer.

I had to do something.

If only I could figure out what.

DGeary	Just heard about Design Your Dreams. Sign me up!
VTalbot	I can use the help. Need to get a group together. This kind of gig is all new to Spencer. Planning starts asap.
DGeary	You do so much for this school.
VTalbot	It's nothing.
DGeary	Better make sure our royal exchange student is on the list.
VTalbot	Ha ha. She's not royal. She's only a Lady, not an HRH.

DGeary   Whatever. But Dani's cousin said that some Brit pop
             star told her that Lady L's mom is all kiss-kiss with John
             Galliano.

VTalbot ::sigh:: So?

DGeary   So if LL gets some visibility, we could get some fabu Dior
             swag, girl! And the Euro and Brit papers would pick it
             up. Think how that would look on the old college apps.

VTalbot I can get into any school I want without asking her for
             anything. Don't you have anything better to do than
             annoy me?

BY THE END of the week, I still hadn't come up with any good
ideas. Meantime, the news about Mac had infiltrated the entire
school, even the maintenance staff, whom I overheard talking
about it in Spanish in the girls' bathroom. I couldn't imagine
why they would care—or maybe they just made a habit of talking
about the students when they thought no one was listening.

I walked across the playing field on my way back from the
field house, where I could watch the girls' soccer practice from
the dance studio's big windows. I'd opted out of team sports this
term and had chosen dance instead, the better to control my
muscle tone. When Emily Overton caught up to me, I thought
she was trying to brush past, which was a little weird considering
there was, like, an acre of grass around us.

"Hi." She sounded a little breathless. "Good game, huh?"

I nodded cautiously. This was the first time in, oh, the entire
two-and-one-tenth terms I'd been here that she'd actually spoken to me. "Nice goaltending," I said. "Especially on that last
shot. I thought for sure their forward would bend it past you."

Emily smiled with modesty that looked real enough. "Parker
always sends it to the top right corner. I had her pegged as soon
as she started for me."

I fell silent, unsure what had brought on this burst of team spirit when I wasn't even on the team.

"So," she said, "you probably don't know this, but I'm on the DYD committee. You know, the charity fashion show in June. I'm helping Vanessa recruit people to help."

"Oh?" I'd been wracking my brain trying to come up with a way to get myself on the committee—because, of course, you didn't just volunteer. If Vanessa was running things, you had to be chosen from among her circle. I'd come up with and discarded half a dozen ways to manipulate her into choosing me, but in the light of day I'd been forced to conclude that none of them would really work.

"Interested in joining us?"

I stared at her. Had I slipped into an alternate universe where gifts just fell out of the sky? Where I, too, was popular and did high-visibility things like organize school events? "Joining you?"

"Sure." When I still couldn't get my mouth to work, she went on, "There are perks to it, of course."

I managed not to laugh—she obviously thought I had to be sold. I was just trying to think of a way to say yes without blubbering in gratitude.

"Besides modeling the clothes, I mean. For one, we get to keep them if we want. And you meet the designers personally at a reception before the show. We all get free tickets. And best of all, Curzon has agreed to let us skip Life Sciences for the term and get five community service credits, as long as we're working on show stuff."

Life Sciences. That was Spencerese for things like Cordon Bleu cookery classes, interior decorating, and fashion design. But wait—how could I give that up when I needed every class to produce a dress for the show? "Do you have to skip?" I asked. "I mean, I've been taking Fashion Design as my elective all year and I really like it."

"You do?" She looked at me as if I'd said I enjoyed trimming my nails with pinking shears.

Not for anything would I tell her my plans. "Yeah. I'm going to be Penny Rose's assistant someday. It's good training."

"Whatever. No, you don't have to skip, but you do need to come to the official committee meetings. Vanessa and DeLayne have already contacted a lot of the designers—and of course hardly anyone is saying no—but now we have to start doing actual work, like hiring an event planner to put together the reception. That kind of stuff." She made a production of fanning her face. "Fund-raising and charity work are a total grind. With the Benefactors' Day thing last fall, we were working on it during summer vacation."

"It's probably not a grind for the people the money goes to." She stared at me blankly. I went on casually, "Who's on the committee so far? Vanessa's friends? The boys, too?"

She nodded. "The boys are ushers for the regents and college scouts who are in town for grad week. It's okay if they have dates—mostly they just show people where to go and then take off. But I know Brett and Rory will come once in a while. They're not stupid. They like a free credit as much as anyone."

This was a total no-brainer. "I'd love to help out. Thanks for inviting me."

She grinned. "Great!" We had nearly reached the main building. "Oh, one more thing. Not that we wouldn't love to have you, but it is sort of conditional."

A chill ran through my stomach. "What, like I have to audition?" I could come up with some design sketches, if that's what she meant.

"No, like you can be on the organizing committee after you do one thing."

"Whatever it is, I can do it."

"Good attitude. We need you to get Lady Lindsay to join us,

too. In fact, Vanessa wants her to be the public face of the show. You know, dialing it up and giving it the whole international aspect. Not just local Californians making good. This is going to be big."

"Oh." The sound I heard was the crash of my expectations and hopes tumbling down around me. "Doesn't Vanessa want to be the face of it? Her family is about as international as it gets."

"Uh-uh." Emily's eyes widened. "She wants to spread the visibility around. She's happy to work behind the scenes—and, of course, she'll be one of the models."

I translated: The event would be huge—which meant that if things went wrong, they'd go wrong on a massive scale, and Vanessa wanted Mac to be stuck with the public humiliation. "I'll ask her when I see her."

No matter what her motivation was, one thing I knew: Vanessa was too proud to admit she'd picked the wrong person to alienate. Such a social faux pas, treating a titled British girl the way she had. So to fix the problem, they had to use an intermediary. A neutral party.

Lucky me.

chapter 4

SAYING YES to whatever they wanted was the easy part.
Asking Mac if she'd be interested in being the "face" of
Design Your Dreams was, well, asking for a helping of
humiliation with a side of sarcasm.

I must have been insane to agree to this. But if it meant my
being on the committee, I'd do it—and more.

After dinner, I went back to my—sorry, *our*—room to work. I
was barely holding my own in AP Chem, and that was only because Gillian was my lab partner. After I finished the two dozen
word problems Mr. Jackson, the math instructor, had assigned,
I read over my chem notes one more time. Don't ask me how
I placed into an AP class. It must have been a computer error.
And with the workload, I'd have to kiss good-bye my plan to be
a tutor. In any case, I'd managed to survive this far, and I was
determined to finish out the year so I could spend my senior
year in nice, low-stress biology, taking lots of lovely design and
history electives as my reward.

Ms. Tobin called lights-out, and Mac had not yet appeared.
I shook my head and closed out of the school's chemistry wiki,

flipping instead to a Bible site on the Web. I didn't actually own a Bible yet. I suppose I could have borrowed one from the school library, assuming they could locate it, or ordered one online. But for now, it was just as easy to go to the study site I'd found. That way, I got a lot of stuff explained without having to reveal to Gillian and Lissa how little I knew about the choice I'd made.

At a quarter to eleven, the door opened and Mac slipped inside.

I looked up. "Any sign of Ms. Tobin?"

A flick of her lashes in my direction. "Any reason there should be?"

"If she catches you out and about after she calls lights-out, it's a demerit."

"What a bore."

My cheeks stung as if she'd slapped them. Why did I even try? "Just thought you should know."

"I did read the manual, Carrie. I'm not completely ignorant. I'm just not interested."

"It's *Carly*. Try to drum up enough interest to remember that." I blinked. Where had *that* come from? Usually I'm better at keeping a zipper on my mouth. The less the general population around here knows about me, the better chance I have of getting the grades I need, bagging my diploma, and getting on with my life. Excepting, of course, my friends and Brett. And Mac was neither.

I braced myself for the inevitable annihilation, but to my surprise she met my gaze full on. "I'm sorry. Carly." Her cheeks, which had been flushed, paled a little. "My best friend at home is Carrie. Caroline, actually. She has dark hair, too."

Silence fell, as long as a breath. "My real name is Carolina," I said, almost afraid to return a personal snippet of information. "So I guess it's an easy slip of the tongue. You probably miss her."

"Thank goodness for Skype." She glanced at me again as she began to get ready for bed. "That's where I've been. In the computer lab, sitting in the dark with the headphones on. Carrie's just about to go to school."

"Lissa's dad is doing post-production on a movie over there, so they do the same thing." I paused. "I think they were shooting at Strathcairn in the winter."

"Were they?"

"She said they were using your castle as a set or something."

She straightened, and whatever color had been in her face drained away completely. "It's not a *castle*. It's a *house*. That's all."

I couldn't imagine why that would make her mad. "Whatever." Time to change the subject, obviously. "I have a message for you."

"What?" She snatched a fresh towel off the heated drying rack and paused in the doorway to the bathroom.

"We're both invited to be on the organizing committee for the Design Your Dreams fashion show in June." Using as few words as possible, I recapped what Emily had told me. "Let Vanessa know if you're interested. Or I can make sure she gets the message."

"Are you going to do it?"

I was tempted to lie, to say I hadn't decided. To make it look like this really didn't matter to me. But putting on a front might backfire—and besides, a Christian should tell the truth, shouldn't she? Look at Gillian. She puts it right out there, and it's up to you to handle it or not. "Yes, I am. But it's conditional on whether you agree, too."

"What's it got to do with me?"

"They'd like you to be the public face—the visible one running the show. To give it an international flavor. I'm not sure what that means, but that's what they told me."

"I don't understand."

"I guess you have cachet—not to mention connections. Maybe you could get Chanel Couture to send you another dress to wear in the show."

I don't think she heard the joke. She gazed into space, thinking. "And Vanessa is running the committee?"

"She runs most of the social things here. It's a gift."

Mac snorted. "So is social climbing, but you don't get any respect for it."

"Oh, she gets plenty of respect. I'm sure inviting both of us to be on the committee was painful for her."

"Why should asking you be painful?"

Let me count the ways. "I didn't realize she knew I existed. She sent someone else to ask me, anyway. I don't rate a personal invitation."

Standing in the bathroom doorway, she considered me. "Don't run yourself down like that. It isn't right."

"What do you mean?" I didn't care how I got the invitation, as long as I got it. Besides, the less contact I had with Vanessa Talbot, the better off I'd be. She'd cozied up to Lissa during our first term, and look how *that* had turned out.

"If she wants me to be on her committee and run her precious show, she's going to have to ask me herself." Mac went into the bathroom and turned the shower on. "If you demand respect, Carly, you usually get it."

I stared blindly at the screen in my lap as the shower began to run. The last thing anybody in their right mind should want is Vanessa Talbot's respect.

✉

To: caragon@spenceracad.edu
From: alanaah@mac.com
Date: April 13, 2009
Re: Hey

Hey little sister, how's it going? Dad told me term started last week. Only three months to go and you're free for summer vacay.

I probably won't be able to get away. Jorge and T-Bone McKay (remember I met him at SXSW last year?) asked me to be the assistant sound designer on Robert Earl Keen's new album. This is major exposure! I haven't said yes yet, but only because I want to make sure I don't scream like a groupie when I talk to them.

How are things with those *gringa* girlfriends of yours? Any sewing projects, or are you too busy with boyfriends and fancy dances?

I had words with Dad about sending you up there all by yourself when you could have come and lived with me. What do you think? Senior year in public school in Austin or maybe even Nashville with your family, like a normal person? Just throwing it out there.

Ti hermana,
Alana

ONLY PEOPLE WHO had earls for grandfathers would expect Vanessa to come to them. People who had prune-pickers for grandfathers usually took a more practical stand. As in, shut up and be grateful you got to be on the committee at all. Anything else was pure gravy.

Unfortunately, I couldn't allow Mac to wait for Vanessa to climb down off her marble plinth and issue a personal invitation. No more keeping my head down and going with the flow. I had to make sure Mac got on that committee, no matter how angry it made me to think about what she'd said. Easy for her to expect people to respect her. That meant they *saw* her first. Visibility was not Mac's problem. It was mine.

But things were about to change. I'd be visible. Oh, yeah. I was going to walk down that runway in the dream dress of the year, and everyone would sit up and open their eyes then. After I got Mac taken care of, I had exactly nine weeks to make it happen.

I speed-dialed my father's number at work and got his assistant. "Ocean Technology Procurement, Mr. Aragon's office."

"Hi, Marina, it's Carly. Does Papa have a second to talk?"

"Hi, sweetie. Your timing is perfect. His nine o'clock just left and his ten hasn't shown yet."

"And I have a class in ten minutes, so I won't hold him up when he does show."

"I've trained you well. Here you go."

My father came on in less than five seconds. "Carly, this is a surprise. Is everything all right?"

"Of course, Papa. But I just need to know . . . I've been invited to be on the committee that is putting together a big fashion show in June. For charity." In case he thought I was wasting my time with extracurriculars, I added, "And I get five community service credits."

"Good for you! Congratulations."

"Thanks. But the deal is, I'll need a dress for the show."

"Didn't you just get one? That pink one you wore on Benefactors' Day?"

"Papa, it's not like that."

"Why not? You didn't spill anything on it, did you?"

"No, I mean I need to make a dress to enter. I'm not sure if it's being judged or not, but I do know it will help me get an internship this summer."

"*Mi corazón*, you don't need to waste your time on a summer job that doesn't pay. And you know I can't shell out for extras like dresses. Heaven help me, I couldn't even give you a *quinceañera* last year. Your Tía Margarita still isn't speaking to me. And then after I paid your friend back—"

"What?" My mouth hung open on the word.

"Of course I couldn't let her buy your clothes for you. I weaseled the information out of her before we left that evening and paid her back."

Lissa had never said a word to me. For two terms now I'd been wracking my brains trying to think of how I could do something for her that equaled her buying half of the evening dress we'd found in the garment district last October. So far I'd come up with nothing. What do you get the girl whose mother's family owns the biggest shopping center in Southern California?

"Papa, I wish you'd have let me take care of it."

"How would you do that, *mi'ja*? You'd have to own your own company to afford the kinds of things your friends have."

"Maybe, but at least I wouldn't have to burden you with it."

I blinked at myself. That was it. I'd get a job. I'd do something that would net me the best fabric money could buy. The fabric would help me decide on a design. Because I'd do it myself, no one would feel sorry for me. And most important, I wouldn't feel this burning sense of obligation toward people I loved, but who didn't understand how it felt to want everything and have nothing.

And don't even get me started on my *quince*. I'm so over it.

"So, now that clothes are out of the way, what else can I do for you?" my father asked, clearly with one eye on the clock.

"Oh, nothing, Papa. I just wanted to know if there was anything extra in the kitty. So since there isn't, I'll go to Plan B."

"Okay, *mi'ja*. See you Friday night."

"'Bye, Papa. *Te amo*."

"I love you, too."

I flipped my phone shut and grabbed my backpack (Prada, half-price off eBay). As soon as classes were over, I would jump onto Craigslist and scan the job boards. While I waited the day or two it would take to get my applications processed, I'd come up with a design for a dress that would drop jaws and incite major envy. And once I had the job, I'd give up trips to restaurants and do my laundry myself, which would give me even more money toward fabric. To get something really amazing, I'd have to order it from London or Milan, and it would cost a hundred bucks a yard, at least. Maybe no one from school would know that, but the designers sitting in the audience sure would. They knew you had to put quality materials in to get a quality garment. So, figure eight yards for a floor-length gown, plus trim at fifty dollars a foot, plus interfacing and lining, not to mention underthings like a corset bra, and we were talking a major investment.

Nine weeks.

I was burning daylight.

EMILY, GOOD LITTLE MESSENGER that she was, found me in the library during third period on Thursday. Maybe she had free period then, too. Or maybe it hadn't occurred to her to go to class. I wasn't sure.

"Hey." She dimpled at me as she let her bag slide to the floor next to where I stood in the stacks, scanning the spines of books with titles like *The Heights of Fashion, 1880–1920* and *Poiret: Designing Art Deco*. "What are you doing?"

"Looking for inspiration," I said absently. The Poiret had some possibilities, but any dress inspired by him meant panels of beading and tons of embroidery. I didn't have time for that.

Emily shot the books a wary glance. "So, did you talk to your roomie about joining us on the committee?"

"I did."

"And? Is she interested? We can't wait around all week, you know. We have to get this going."

I took a breath. "She wants to talk with Vanessa about it personally. It's a big commitment."

"Personally?"

"Yes. You know, in case she has questions."

"What questions? We're organizing a fashion show. How many questions can there be?"

"Mac has some."

Emily leaned in and dropped her voice. "Do you call her Lady Lindsay? You don't have to curtsy, do you?"

I stared at her. "She isn't the queen. And no, I call her Mac, like she asked me to."

"What's she like? I mean, I kind of feel sorry for you, having to room with her. Does she make you do her laundry?"

Was it possible for anyone to be this offensive and not know it? "She's different," I said coldly. "And the service does her laundry, same as the rest of us." *You nitwit*, my tone said. Only I'd be doing my own down in the basement, starting this week. I'd already sent a note to Mrs. Dumfries asking if I could have this term's fee refunded, since it came out of my pocket money.

I reshelved the books and grabbed a couple of volumes of *Women's Wear Daily* to page through in my room. "Anyway, let Vanessa know Mac wants to talk to her, would you? I have to go."

As I headed for the circulation desk, I could hear the sound of French tips on a keypad. We weren't allowed to use cell phones in the library, but Mrs. Lynn evidently hadn't caught on to texting yet.

TEXT MESSAGE

Emily Overton	I just talked to Carly and she says LL wants a personal invite.
Vanessa Talbot	Why?
Emily Overton	In case she has questions.
Vanessa Talbot	You told her no?
Emily Overton	No.
Vanessa Talbot	No what?
Emily Overton	No I didn't tell her no.
Vanessa Talbot	I may want her on the committee but I don't have to talk to her!
Emily Overton	??
Vanessa Talbot	Never mind.

✉

To: DList_DYD_Committee
From: VTalbot@spenceracad.edu
Date: April 16, 2009
Re: Kickoff meeting tonight

We'll have our first official meeting with everyone on the committee tonight at 8:00 at TouTou's. I've reserved the private room upstairs, desserts and beverages only.

We'll welcome our new members Parker Potrero, Carly Aragon, and Lindsay MacPhail, as well as senior class liaison Summer Fremont.

Remember, our job is to make this the biggest event the San Francisco fashion world has seen in years. But no pressure :)

Until tonight,
Vanessa
....

AT DINNER, I sat with Lissa and Shani and picked at my risotto. "I don't think it's worth it," I told them. "I don't know about getting between Mac and Vanessa, even if seeing Brett is one of the perks." It was safer to let them think I was motivated by that. I was almost afraid to tell my friends about my bigger dreams. I didn't want to jinx them. I was sure that just because I wanted to be in the show so badly, someone would take it away from me.

"It's like what Dr. Ellis was talking about in history class," Shani said. "The Wars of the Roses."

I didn't quite make the connection, but I got the war part.

"Can't you just be on the committee and let Mac do whatever she's going to do?" Lissa asked.

"I'm her roommate," I pointed out. "And let's face it—they only want me if they get her."

Lissa speared a mushroom. "On the other hand, if Vanessa caves and you're Mac's friend, that could be a good thing. The girl could use some competition."

"I'm not into competition," I protested. "But I do want to work with Brett. Why does it have to be so complicated?"

Neither of them had an answer for me. And I still didn't know what I was going to do when I slipped into our room and found Mac there, snacking on a bag of chips (or crisps, as she called them) and reading her e-mail.

She frowned at a message, swore under her breath, and stabbed it out of existence with one perfectly manicured nail.

She opened another one, scanned it, and looked up, her forehead still creased.

"The Talbot requests our presence at someplace called Tou-Tou's at eight," she informed me. "Any idea where or what that is?"

"It's a hundred and fifty a plate, is what it is," I replied, sinking onto my bed. Okay, so the timing wasn't great. She seemed ticked about something. But I needed to convince her to come. If she and Vanessa worked out their differences, I'd have met the condition and would be safely on the committee. "You'd probably enjoy it."

"It takes a bit more than that." She took a breath and the frown smoothed out. "Well, it's drinks and dessert, apparently. I do hope a meeting is optional."

Did that mean she would go? "You wanted to talk it over with Vanessa in person. That would be a good time to do it."

"And perhaps there will be chocolate," she said, as if she was adding up the pros and cons. Maybe there was hope.

"And I'd like it if you came." Nothing like putting yourself right out there. I was getting good at this. Well, she could choose to flatten me again if she wanted. At least I was trying.

"Why?" Mac looked at me curiously.

"They . . . well, they're not exactly my crowd."

"So why go?"

"Because they invited us? And because I assume I have some kind of job to do?"

"I think there's more to it than that." She waited, but I buttoned my lip and resisted the urge to say, "Because I need your help. Because I have plans for my life, and this is one way to put them in motion. And because there are perks—maybe if I were friends with you, Brett would notice I was there."

Uh-huh. Dream on, Carly. Anyone standing next to Lady Lindsay MacPhail disappears into the wallpaper, never to be seen again.

Mac got to her feet. "All right. I'll come with you. On one condition."

Of course. How could I have expected anything less? "What?"

"You introduce me to that dishy lad with the dark eyes."

Cold horror splashed into my stomach. "Which one?"

"You can hardly miss him. His equally dishy blond friend who insists on hanging around with Vanessa called him Brett."

I dragged air into lungs that had quit wanting to work. "Sure," I said in a completely beige tone. "I'd be happy to."

She could get me what I wanted—a place on the committee. Too bad she could also take what I wanted—Brett. Achieving one dream would be pretty empty without the other.

chapter 5

TOUTOU'S. None of my friends had ever been there; Gillian had gotten close once, but the ratball who'd been her date had stood her up. It didn't look all that much different from your average San Francisco bistro—lots of glossy wood and glass and orchids—until you noticed Robin Williams having dinner with his wife at the window table. Or Kate and Laura Mulleavy laughing together over drinks. Or the rented sedan with the long telephoto lens hanging out of the driver's side on the opposite side of the street.

Of course Vanessa and her gang would choose to hang out there.

I dressed carefully, even running down to Gillian to beg for her blue silk Bottega Veneta swing jacket. It went perfectly with the Hanni Y. silver-and-white silk polka-dot dress I'd nabbed on sale at Bloomie's in Palo Alto just before school started. I pinned my mop of hair up into a loose French twist and was feeling pretty good about my look when Mac stepped out of the bathroom.

In a Prada glazed-ice minidress I'd seen pictures of from the Milan shows.

It was already ten to eight, so there was no time for me to

change or even to think about it. Oh, who was I fooling—I had nothing to change into anyway.

Cabs typically cruised the street at the end of the driveway after school hours, so we walked across the lawn to flag one. "Oh, please," Mac muttered as a photographer leaning on the wrought-iron fence straightened and scrutinized us. Next to him was a skinny guy in a gray hoodie who whipped out a cheap little camera and snapped a picture. That couldn't be a pro. It feels a little weird to go to a school that's on the tourist radar. I turned my back, searching the street for a cab.

"Don't bother," the older guy muttered. "She's nobody."

Nobody? I tried not to laugh as Mac averted her face, too.

"The dark one, maybe, but the redhead's Lady—" the younger guy began, but a cab slid up to the curb. High heels and all, we ran for it and I didn't hear the rest. We made it to the restaurant ten minutes late, with me following Mac up the stairs, feeling like a seven-year-old in my polka dots.

Everyone else was already there.

Chin up, girlfriend. So what if the paparazzi don't care who you are? You're still not sliding in behind her.

This was a make-or-break moment. If I started off in Mac's shadow, I may as well cut a rent check and stay there. So when she stepped into the room hips first, in her model-like way, I did the same. I even stepped around her, greeting Vanessa and Emily with air kisses and that brush of arms that passes for a hug.

A cool, noncommittal smile tilting her mouth, Mac let me introduce her to as many people as I knew, and I tried to remember the names of the ones I didn't as they introduced themselves. And then came the moment I'd been dreading behind my polka dots and bright smile.

"Mac," I said steadily, "this is Brett Loyola, who's in AP Chem with me. Brett, this is my roommate, Lindsay MacPhail, but she goes by Mac."

"Nice to meet you." The sexy grin Brett shot her would have made my knees dissolve if it had been directed at me.

And then it was. Directed at me, I mean. I think I actually forgot to breathe.

"What did you say your name was?" he asked.

Oh Lord, take me now. A heart attack would be good. With an ambulance and a teary deathbed good-bye that would wipe out the utter humiliation of this moment.

"It's Carly Aragon," Mac said smoothly. "I do like all my friends to know each other."

"Does that mean I get to be your friend?" he asked, with the kind of smile that already knows the answer.

"We'll see."

He grinned even wider at the promise in her tone. "Come on. Why don't you join me and Cal?"

I didn't stop to wonder if the "you" was singular or plural. I just went. This time last week, I'd have laughed if you'd told me I'd be sitting at a table in TouTou's with Lissa's ex, Callum McCloud, and Brett Loyola. It would have ranked right up there with winning *Project Runway* or getting an offer to intern with Tori Wu, who designs Gillian's party dresses. Instead, I smiled and ate chocolate torte and drank a virgin peach bellini (much to everyone's amusement—how much did they bribe the management to serve all these pretty martinis to minors?) and felt like I was cracking wide open inside.

"All right, everyone," Vanessa said, when we all had drinks and dessert, "I'm calling this meeting to order."

"Do you have to?" Callum called. "Bo-o-ring."

"You know the rules. We have to at least say the words *charity fashion show.*"

"Charity fashion show!" half a dozen people chanted helpfully. "Can we have another drink now?"

"No," she said. "Work first. I want to get people on task, and then you're free to do whatever you want."

Despite their moaning and groaning, it went pretty smoothly—until Vanessa got to Mac. "Lady Lindsay, I'm so glad you came. Your job will be the best of all." She leaned, all chummy, on Callum's arm as he half-sat, half-stood on the long-legged stool. Unlike me. My feet dangled inches above the floor.

"As far as I know, I haven't agreed to any sort of job." Mac took another bite of her olallieberry and amaretto parfait. "Since I wasn't actually asked."

"Emily asked you."

"Check your facts. Emily asked Carly."

"And Carly must have asked you, since you're here. Which is good enough for me. Now, let me brief you on what we're going to need."

"I'd prefer to be invited personally, which I believe I made clear."

Vanessa sighed and rolled her eyes, her whole body demanding, "What did I do to deserve such a diva?"

I sat, frozen, watching as my one chance to get on the committee wobbled like a high-wire act between two opposing wills. *Just give in. Don't do this to me.* Maybe I should have taken the risk and told Mac what this meant to me.

"Lady Lindsay, don't you think you're overworking this?"

"Please stop calling me that."

"It's your name, isn't it?"

"I prefer Mac. Less pretentious."

"Pretentious," Vanessa repeated, as if to say, *you're worried about your name? What about your whole attitude?*

I resisted the urge to bury my face in my hands.

"Mm." Mac spooned up a berry and regarded it with interest. "These are lovely. What do you suppose they're called?"

Social conversation was not on Vanessa's menu. "I'm giving you what amounts to the chair. It's going to be your face in the magazines and on the advertising. People would kill for this. Are you going to help or not?"

"Is that a personal invitation?"

From the depths of my despair, I had to hand it to Mac. She had actually challenged Vanessa in public. Imagine having that much confidence—not to mention the skill to turn a room that belonged to Vanessa into an arena where whatever she did, Vanessa would lose.

"Oh, give it a rest," Vanessa snapped. "*Yes*, if that's what it takes to get some help."

"Thank you. I'd love to." Mac smiled as though she'd just been handed a present, all tied up in glossy ribbon. "How kind of you to include me."

Vanessa snorted. "I hope you don't plan to be such a b—I mean, be this difficult with everything. Your job is the most important and visible of all."

"So I understand. I'm delighted."

"Now that that's over, can we get another drink?" Brett complained. As Vanessa tossed her hair back and walked away, a server materialized to take his order, and Brett glanced at the rest of us at the table. "Anyone else?"

"A cinnamon latte, please," I said.

"Coffee?" He sounded like I'd asked for motor oil. "Why don't you get a real drink—not one of those mocktails you had before. The girls tell me the Cosmos are good here."

"I'd love one," Mac said.

I opened my mouth, but before I could say anything, Brett glanced at the server. "Two Cosmos and two Stellas."

"Certainly, Mr. Loyola," the guy said, and vanished.

Problem. Last week I'd have shrugged and spent the whole evening nursing it, since it was Brett who'd ordered it for me and I didn't want to look like a complete prudie in front of him. But last week I hadn't made a certain life-changing choice that meant I'd have to make other choices, even if they were just little ones. Like now.

The server put the drinks, decorated with paper-thin orange slices, in front of us with a flourish. I took a breath and pushed mine back toward him. "I ordered a latte, please. Cinnamon."

"I beg your pardon, miss. I'll be right back."

Brett turned to me, puzzled. "Is something wrong with it?"

"No, I'm sure it's great." I smiled, amazed that I was sitting across from him and he was actually saying something more than "Can I borrow your notes?" I went on, "But I ordered a latte. I guess he didn't hear me."

"I ordered this for you." He actually looked hurt, and my heart melted. I'd only just gotten him to see me. It was a little too much to expect that he'd listen to me as well.

"Thank you. But I don't drink."

"Oh, come on, Carmen. Grow up."

"My name is Carly."

"Oh, right. Sorry. You're in my chem class."

And you've borrowed my notes a hundred times. "Yes."

"You look different." Again that smile, deep and dark. "Nice."

"Th-thanks," I managed, blinking in the warmth of those eyes. Who cared about drinks? Was this really happening? *Breathe. Take a breath.*

The table was tiny and he sat close enough that I could smell his cologne. Spice and a hint of musk and lemon. I had no idea what it was called, but I was going to haunt the men's counter at Nordstrom until I found out.

His gaze panned sideways. "So. Mac. What brings you to our town?"

"I'm an exchange student." Did she have to lock eyes with him like that? Couldn't she just make small talk like a normal person? "I'm here for the term, and then I'm going to the back of beyond for the summer. Maybe. "

"The back of where?" Callum asked.

"Someplace called Alberta. Apparently the Prince of Wales owned a ranch there in the thirties and they want me to work with the horses. Take people on riding tours. That sort of thing."

"Sounds wonderful," I said. How did people find jobs like this? I'd been doing searches daily on Craigslist and hadn't turned up anything I could do outside of class time.

"I don't know," she said, dabbing her orange slice into her Cosmo. "My father set it up. I may just bag it and volunteer on the *Lady Washington* for a couple of months. Or go to Provence and do *plein air* watercolors. It's impossible to make a decision."

"I dunno, working on a ranch sounds cool." Brett's eyes were filled with interest. "What do you know about horses?"

She shrugged. "I have a couple at home in Scotland."

"There you go. Horses instead of Provence or the sailing ship. Easy choice."

"I'd go to Paris," I heard myself say. "I'd intern at Dior, picking up fabric scraps just to work in haute couture."

"Oat couture?" Callum pretended to look puzzled. "What's that? Food for high-class horses?"

Mac rolled her eyes while I hung onto my opportunity to speak. "I'm into design, and Paris and New York would be my top two choices. That, or trying to get into one of the studios in L.A. Movie costuming would be really cool."

"So what do you think of Spencer so far?" Brett asked Mac.

I felt the animation fade from my face as I realized he was more interested in hearing about Mac than me. Okay. Fine. Clearly I needed to find a topic that would catch a guy's attention. What had I been thinking? Of course clothes and fabrics weren't going to do that.

"It's all right," Mac answered. "Different."

"Different how?" Brett wanted to know.

She shrugged. "Chemistry is all right. But I had some of the maths last year. And I suppose English is English wherever you go."

"What's your best subject?" I asked. If they wanted to make small talk, I could do that.

"None of them." The boys laughed as if that was funny.

I felt like shrinking away. Why couldn't I be like Gillian, who could gather an audience just by opening her mouth? Or like Shani, who said whatever she wanted to and couldn't care less what people thought? She'd make short work of this crowd, that was for sure. "You people need to get a *life*," she'd say. Something I'd never have the guts to do, even if it was the truth.

"Everyone enjoying themselves?" I looked up as Vanessa hooked an empty stool with her high-heeled foot and slid it over. The girl who'd been sitting there was going to have to fend for herself when she got back from the bathroom.

"Sure." Callum hitched his own stool to the right a couple inches so she could join us.

"Lovely," Mac agreed. "I now have a new favorite drink." She toasted Vanessa with her Cosmo and took a sip.

"Whose is this?" Vanessa tapped the second one with a fingernail.

"Hers, but she doesn't want it," Brett said with a glance at me.

"What's the matter with it?"

I couldn't remember Vanessa ever looking at me directly before. It's not the kind of thing you want to encourage. I shrugged. "I don't drink."

"Poor you." Vanessa waved at the waiter and handed it to him. "I'll have one of these, please. So, Lad—er, Mac, I'm looking forward to working with you."

"Yes, I'm sure we're going to be the best of friends."

Vanessa shot her a glance. Even I couldn't tell if Mac was being sarcastic or sincere. Some people just have a gift.

"I think so, too. Why don't you come with us this weekend? I can brief you on the high points then. We're all going up to Napa to stay at Brett's winery."

Brett looked down modestly. "It's not really mine. It's the family's. But it'd be great if you came. It'll be fun."

If those puppy-dog eyes had been focused on me, I'd have promised him the moon and anything else he wanted.

But they weren't.

Mac smiled back. "What do you do there? Tasting?"

Vanessa nodded. "That, and shopping, and the boys take their dirt bikes up into the hills."

"Really?" For the first time, Mac looked interested. "That sounds like fun."

"The shopping in Napa isn't *that* great," Vanessa began, but Mac cut her off.

"I didn't mean that. I meant the dirt bikes. What kind do you have?"

"Honda five hundreds."

"I've not ridden anything bigger than a two-fifty."

"I'll be happy to show you, then." Brett's smile would have melted chocolate.

Mac's would have made it boil.

I just sat there. I doubted I'd ever be warm again.

chapter 6

"YOU'D BETTER WATCH YOURSELF."

Mac hung the Prada—carefully, I was relieved to note—in her wardrobe. I put away my own dress and hung Gillian's jacket from the top drawer handle of my dresser, ready to give to her in the morning. We'd made it back just in time for lights-out, and I didn't want to risk running into Ms. Tobin in the corridor or on the stairs.

"What do you mean?"

She sat on the bed and I could feel her gaze under my skin, seeing right into my mind. "You look at him and it shows all over your face. He doesn't know, but you can bet Vanessa does."

"I don't know what you're talking about," I mumbled as I dashed into the bathroom to hide my burning face.

"All right," she called equably. "Have it your way."

"It doesn't matter anyhow." The words forced themselves out, despite the fact that they had to contend with a toothbrush and toothpaste. "When he looks at the two of us, all he sees is you."

"Do you think so?"

She leaned on the bathroom door jamb as I bent over the

sink to spit. "I know so. And since you brought it up, so does Vanessa."

"I thought they'd broken up."

"They have. But that doesn't mean she'll let the competition have him." I rinsed my mouth. "At least your chances are better than mine."

"What makes you say that?"

I shrugged. She was the daughter of an earl. I was a scholarship student. She wore Prada. I wore last season's sale finds or whatever I could borrow. If she couldn't figure that out, she was a lot slower on the uptake than I'd given her credit for.

"Of the two of us, I'd say you're more his type," she mused. "I mean, look at me. Hair like a dynamite explosion. Eyebrows I have to color in every day with an eyebrow pencil. Freckles. Now look at you. Gorgeous hair, a bum that would make Shakira jealous, and skin that behaves. I mean, seriously."

Heat scalded my face. "That's the problem. He doesn't look at me. Or if he does, he sees a disembodied hand holding out chemistry notes and that's it." I pushed past her. "I don't want to talk about it. If he likes you, you're welcome to him."

"Thanks so much. But you should do something about that."

"What?"

"I don't know. A girl like you should have more self-confidence."

"A girl like me." What did that mean? "I have lots of self-confidence."

"What you have is this uncanny ability to disappear in full view."

"Huh?" In spite of myself, I came back to stand in the bathroom doorway.

"I saw it." She got her toothpaste out of her side of the cabinet and began to brush her teeth. "One minute you were there, and the next you weren't. So Brett and Callum spent the rest of the evening talking to me. You only came back into view when you left. And by the way, no thanks for ditching me. I was forced to walk back with Vanessa and Dani whats-her-name."

"You guys were having a good time." I could hardly string the words together, I was so taken aback by what she thought of me. "Besides, Brett would have walked you back, I'm sure."

She finished brushing and reached for a towel. "Right. Well. He didn't. He's a day student, so he went rabbiting off up the hill with Callum, and somehow I wound up with The Talbot and Dani. Goodness, that cousin of hers is tiresome. I'm never buying another album again."

I had to smile. "I don't think it's the cousin who's tiresome. I think it's the endless repetition of stories about her that is. Poor Dani. She needs a life so bad."

"Well, I'm not a charity. She'll have to find a life on her own. And we were talking about you."

"No, we weren't." I climbed into bed. "Subject closed. Maybe my friends can say things like that to me"—in fact, they probably would— "but I'm not ready to hear them from anyone else."

"So I'm not your friend, then."

I didn't know how to answer that, so I didn't say anything.

She waited a second, then turned on her iPod, settling into her pillows with her earphones in. She didn't look at me again.

I climbed into bed and flipped open my laptop, looking for the chapter in Romans I'd been reading the night before. Looking for a little comfort. A little reassurance.

Because something in the silence told me I'd just made a very big mistake.

MAC DIDN'T WASTE a single word on me the next day.

You'd think I'd have been happy about this, but to be honest, it only made the tension in our room ratchet higher. How awkward was it to be sitting at the desk on the other side of the room and hear her make a muffled growl and stab another e-mail into nonexistence, knowing that I should ask, "Everything okay?" knowing at the same time that she'd just snap at me or, worse, ignore me.

Apparently my window of forgiveness had closed. The window between Mac and Vanessa, though, was wide open. Vanessa seemed to be listening to that guy who once said you should keep your friends close but your enemies closer, because she and Mac had become BFFs overnight. I had no idea how Mac could do this without seeing through her the way she saw through me, but there you were. The worst of it came that night.

I was packing my overnight bag before Enrique and the limo arrived to get me at six. The door burst open and Mac and Vanessa came in on a rush of perfume and chatter.

"I have no idea what to wear," Mac wailed, throwing open the door of her wardrobe. "Look at this. Not one winery-friendly outfit."

"It's not like you're going to be stomping grapes yourself." Vanessa began to pull things off their hangers. "This is good. And this. Ooh, cute capris. Those, too. And this and this in case we have a party."

Mac got one of the Vuittons out from under her bed and began stuffing clothes into it. Her trunk and the bigger suitcases had gone into storage downstairs. I assumed there would be someone to press her things when they got to Napa, or maybe Mac just didn't care.

Vanessa tossed a Hermès scarf around her shoulders and glanced into the mirror on the back of the door to see how it went with her frothy silk BCBG sundress. Then she looked over at me and saw the case on the bed. "Oh, I didn't realize you were planning to come, too."

"She's not." Makeup rattled against the counter in the bathroom. "At least, I don't think so." Mac stuck her head out the bathroom door. "Are you?"

It was the first thing she'd said directly to me since yesterday. That must have been what startled me into replying. "Of course not."

Vanessa raised an eyebrow at my tone. "Something better to do?"

"My father sends a car every Friday to take me home."

"But Brett invited you, didn't he?"

"I think he invited Mac. I hope you have a great time."

"I'm sure I shall." Mac came out of the bathroom with her toiletries case and tucked it into the bag, then zipped it shut. "All ready."

But Vanessa didn't seem to be in any hurry. "I'm just about positive Brett wanted little Carly here to come. How could you want to go home—wherever that is—instead of spending the weekend with all your friends?"

"She's made it clear who her friends are, Van." Mac picked up the bag. "Ready?"

"Has she?" Vanessa hadn't taken her eyes off me. *Back away from the claws and teeth. Slowly.* Problem was, there was nowhere to go except out the window, and we were three floors up. Then she answered her own question. "Oh, I remember now. You hang out with those so-called Christian people, don't you?"

"Yes," I said quietly. *Come on, Enrique. Please don't be late, today of all days.*

"They're too good for the likes of us," I thought Mac said, but I couldn't be sure because she was out in the corridor. What had happened to the girl who tried to encourage me about my looks? And what was this about being too good for her because we were Christians? I'd never once said or done anything to make her feel that way.

Right?

You snubbed her, dummy. Now it's payback time.

Vanessa looked into my overnight case. "How old *is* this?" She held up my silk polka-dot dress, which I'd packed in case Papa took us out to dinner. "This is from, what, the spring before last?"

"It's an old favorite." I resisted the urge to tear it out of her hand and fling it back into the bag. "It's comfortable, so I keep it around."

"Really." Again that heavy-lidded, penetrating stare. "I'll bet you got it on sale somewhere recently. For an old favorite, it's hardly been worn."

"I take care of my stuff."

"Sure you do. I wonder why you bother, though, when you probably got it for half-price." She shuddered. "I'm glad you're not going. If there's anything I can't stand, it's a poser."

I drew myself up to my full five feet two inches. No matter how much I wanted to zing her with something withering, I couldn't do it. For one thing, zinging her would put me on her level, and that was the last thing I wanted. And for another, I needed my place on the committee. Only an idiot would risk that just for one second's satisfaction.

But before I could say a word, my phone rang and I snatched it up. "Enrique? Great. I'll be right down." I grabbed my bag. "My limo's here. It's been nice chatting with you. Have a good weekend."

As I practically ran down the corridor, I heard them behind me, giggling and talking in that just-below-audible tone that meant they probably had a few choice things to say about me, my clothes, my family, and my friends.

I didn't care. I didn't. They could say what they wanted, as long as they let me stay on the committee. But Vanessa's spooky ability to put her immaculate nail on those soft, defenseless places where I was most vulnerable had me worried. I needed to toughen up . . . and to become more indispensable. And while I was at it, I needed to get started on my dress. To do that, I had to stop surfing Craigslist and actually get out there and look for a part-time job.

"Hey, *chica*," Enrique said as I opened the rear passenger door. "How's it hanging?"

"Fine." I tossed my bag in and followed it. "Did you see Papa today?"

"Oh, man, that's the problem," he said. "He says to say he's real sorry, but he had to go to Guadalajara. Emergency of some kind. He'll be back Tuesday, but he says you and Antony are to stay with Tía Donna in Saratoga."

He put the car into gear.

"Enrique, wait." He looked over the seat at me. Tía Donna wasn't really my aunt. She was a friend of my mom's, and we stayed there sometimes when Papa had to fly off unexpectedly on our weekends at home. She had three boys, all under fourteen, and while this was great for Antony, there are places I'd rather be than struggling to keep my sanity in the midst of a Halo smackdown.

"If Papa isn't going to be there, I think I'll stay at school this weekend."

"Are you sure, *mi alma*? Because you know Donna. She loves having you guys."

"I know. But it'll be like a holiday for Antony if I'm not there yelling at them all the time, you know? I've got a lot of things to do, and this would be the perfect time to do them."

My cousin shrugged. "Okay, *mi'ja*, if that's what you want. Just call your dad and let him know. I don't want him thinking I ditched you."

"He knows you'd never do that." I leaned over the seat and gave him a kiss on the cheek. "I'm sorry you drove all this way for nothing."

"It wasn't nothing, *mi'ja*, trust me."

I slid out of the long black limo with my bag and slammed the door shut. It purred off down the drive and I slipped inside the big double doors. In less than a minute I'd dashed up two flights of stairs and banged on Lissa and Gillian's door.

"What are you doing here?" Gillian stepped aside as I slipped past her.

"Can I hang here with you for half an hour? Just until the coast is clear?"

"Of course."

"What coast?" Lissa considered a pile of dresses in the middle of her bed. "Since when do you care whether it's clear?"

"I'm avoiding someone. Everyone." The overnight bag was getting heavy. I let it drop to the floor and sank into Gillian's desk chair. "Going somewhere?"

"We're going to try out a new restaurant behind Ghirardelli Square and then catch a movie," Gillian said. "Which means you have to build two hours into the schedule for Lissa to get dressed."

"Not fair," Lissa protested. She grabbed a deceptively simple Chloe linen sundress in a scrumptious raspberry. "I can make up my mind in less than that."

"Only barely." Gillian, looking cool and comfortable in her favorite cropped cargo pants and a piecework camisole, lounged on her bed. "So, Carly, are we going to talk about Lissa's clothes habit, or are you going to tell us why you aren't on your way down to San Jose?"

"Not to mention who you're avoiding." Lissa put in big gold hoop earrings, her blue gaze on me.

"My dad had to go to Guadalajara on some emergency for work, so we're supposed to go to this friend of ours. Except with her kids and my brother, that would be like locking myself in a cage with four orangutans on crack, so I just told the driver

I'd stay here." Should I tell them about my plans to find a job? After a second, I decided against it. The fewer people who knew about my financial status, the better. "I have stuff to do in the city anyway."

"So you're not hiding from your family or your driver," Gillian said. "And you're not hiding from us. Who does that leave?"

"I need to stay out of my room until I know Mac and Vanessa and all their crowd are on the highway to Napa," I said on a rush of breath.

"Did you have a fight?" Count on Lissa to ask. I could probably pick up a few pointers from a pro on fighting with Vanessa.

"Kind of. Mac isn't speaking to me at the moment."

"Why?" Lissa asked.

"I think I hurt her feelings."

"She has feelings?" Gillian looked amazed.

"How could you manage to hurt anyone?" Lissa shook her head. "You're the kindest person I know."

"You must not know very many people, then." My shoulders slumped. "Mac said something about us being friends and I didn't give her an answer. She hasn't spoken to me since. Well, except just now when she and Vanessa came in to pack and we sort of got into it."

"Tell all." Lissa settled in for the show. All that was missing was the popcorn and soda.

I sketched it out for them, and when I was finished, Gillian shook her head. "We might have known she'd gravitate to that crowd. I mean, it was really only a matter of time. I don't think you've lost anything."

"You don't belong with them, Carly." Lissa came to sit beside me and gave me a hug. "You're too nice. Too real. You need to get off that stupid committee before you turn into a pod person."

"A what?"

"You know, those things from *Night of the Living Dead*."

She really needs to stop watching the SciFi channel. "Uh, no."

"Never mind." She shook her hair back. "The point is, we're way more fun than they are, and we don't give a rip what they think. You're coming to dinner with us, right?"

I nodded. I knew who my real friends were. The thing that nagged at me was, I'd just read in my online study that it was better to hang a rock around your neck and throw yourself into the sea than to offend somebody. I'd offended Mac, and the knowledge was just like that rock, weighing me down.

But it would be easier to be chucked into the Pacific to drown than to ask Vanessa Talbot's new BFF to forgive me.

chapter 7

SATURDAY MORNING, I came up with a plan. By nine I'd made it to the dining room for breakfast and back out again with no one seeing me, and by ten I was on the bus. I needed to find a job far enough away from the school so I wouldn't run into anyone I knew, but close enough that it would be easy to get to. The bus was the solution. It stopped just across from the Spencer playing fields and went all the way to Chinatown.

I started there, at Tori Wu's loft, where I'd made an appointment for eleven.

"Carly," she said, shaking hands. "You're Gillian Chang's friend."

"It's nice to see you again," I replied, relieved that she remembered me from when we'd been there in September, buying a Benefactors' Day Ball dress for Gillian. "Thank you for making time for me."

"What can I do for you? A special dress?" She pulled the measuring tape from around her neck and sat, tossing it onto a drafting table behind her. There was no tea and fashion show this time—I was not, after all, Gillian's aunt Isabel, with all the money of the Formosa-Pacific banking family behind me.

"No." I gulped. "I need to find a job to pay for some of my school expenses, and I was wondering if you had an opening." Her lashes flickered with surprise, and I hurried on. "I'm willing to do anything—sweep up scraps, answer the phone, place orders. I've been sewing all my life and I'm taking design classes. See?" I reached into my bag and pulled out a sheaf of spot drawings: a cuff detail, a neckline, a ruffled hem insert.

She riffled through them. "These are yours? Very nice." She looked up. "But I'm afraid I don't have anything open right now. I could use someone this summer, though. My cutter's assistant is going out on maternity leave, if you're interested in applying. You wouldn't get minimum wage. You'd get what the other assistants get."

In spite of my disappointment in the short term, I could hardly believe my luck. "Wow. I—I'd be honored to interview. And I'm hoping to enter a dress in the Design Your Dreams show, if you want to see a sample of my work. Have you heard about it?"

"Oh, yes. They called me last week. I'll look forward to seeing your sample." Her keen glance ran down the front of my jacket with its notched hem that, I realized, had begun with the very drawing she held. "Speaking of samples, you made that jacket."

"Yes. During winter break."

She reached over and held it open with one hand, taking in the collar, the lining, and especially the hem. She could probably tell how hard I'd worked to make the notching lie smooth and flat in both lining and fabric, while the contrast piping stood out the way it should, without bumps or puckers. "Very nice. Be sure to come back when you're out of school, okay? I don't see many students with skill like this. I could teach you a few things that would make these tailoring details easier."

"Thank you! Thanks so much."

I was still reeling from her compliments, even though a summer job was far from a sure thing, as I floated out the door and got back on the bus.

At noon I was still a little delirious as I got off near a *taquería* and got myself a burrito for lunch, liberally laced with hot *chilés de arbol*. By two, my optimism had begun to fade, after half a dozen personal rejections and one proposition by the nasty guy stocking shampoo at the drugstore, and by three, I was trudging up the hot sidewalk, wondering what on earth I was doing this for.

Sure, I wanted to show the people who mattered in the fashion world what I could do. But did I really need imported fabric at a hundred and change a yard? If Tori Wu would interview me on the basis of a few sketches and a jacket, did I need to create a dress and enter the show at all?

Or was it more than the show? *Come on, Carly, have the guts to at least be honest.* I wanted what the show could do for me—over and above an internship. I wanted to walk up to Brett Loyola in a dress that had been photographed for everything from the *Chronicle* to whowhatweardaily.com. I wanted him to see me as a success . . . on my own . . . not just as Mac's roommate. Once he saw me that way, maybe it wouldn't matter to him that I didn't come with a pedigree. I couldn't help it that something about him could make me forget to breathe every time I saw him. Call it chemistry. Call it craziness. But there was no telling my body or my heart to forget about him. I wanted him to see me, and I wanted it to be on *my* terms.

So. Onward.

I'd come halfway back to school and was waiting for the next bus when something caught my eye in the window of the photography shop behind me.

PICCADILLY PHOTO
Help Wanted

The sign was tiny, as if whoever had put it there wasn't sure they wanted help at all. Still, it took about six milliseconds before the bell on the door was jangling behind me. A tall, gray-haired guy who could double for Sir Ian McKellan (See? She may be a lovable dork, but Lissa's movie collection is really rubbing off on me) came out from the back at the sound.

"May I help you?"

He wore a Glengarry plaid vest and faded jeans, and a silk scarf at his wrinkly throat. But his eyes were very kind, and he moved with the dignity of someone who might once have been a soldier.

I took a step forward, hand outstretched. "My name is Carly Aragon, and I'm a junior at Spencer Academy."

"Are you, now?" His grip was strong. Ouch. "Surely they haven't taken to flogging the streets for fund-raising."

I grinned and surreptitiously flexed my fingers. "No, it's just me doing the flogging. I'm looking for a way to pay my school expenses, and I saw your sign in the window."

"Aha. Have you developed photographs before?"

"Um, no."

"Worked behind a counter?"

"No, but I'm in AP Chemistry. It can't be as hard as that." I squelched a flutter of panic at the thought of what Gillian called "thirdterms" next week. Had I done nearly enough studying? No.

"Done any customer service work at all?"

"Just charity events with my mom." Back in the days when having to do something like find a job would never have entered my head.

"Useful experience. What else can you do?"

I thought fast. "I can keep things clean. And smile at people and make them glad they came. I can do math in my head and keep my mouth shut. Oh, and I can make a really good *salsa verde* with avocado and *tomatillos*."

"That will come in very handy in a photography shop, I'm sure."

"It will at lunchtime. I'm good on the computer and I can use Photoshop." Everyone in my design classes could.

"CS2?"

"CS3."

One eyebrow rose. "How soon can you start?"

I gave him my best smile, hoping he wasn't just being rhetorical. "Is right now soon enough?"

After a moment's consideration, he said, "Why don't you fill out an application form so I have the basics, and then you can grab the Swiffer mop from the storeroom and have a go at the floors. There is Windex and a bag of rags for the glass counters. Get this place sparkling by five o'clock and I'll pay you for two hours' work."

I felt like shrieking for joy, but I restrained myself. "What is the pay, exactly?"

I braced myself to hear "minimum wage," but when he named a figure six dollars an hour over that, I had to grip the counter—creating mondo fingerprints I'd have to wipe later—to stop myself from giving him a big hug. "That would be fine," I said in my most businesslike tone. "Thank you. You won't be sorry."

"I trust not." He rummaged under the counter and found an application form that looked as though it had been there a long time. "Once you have the shop mastered—which might take until tomorrow—I'll show you how the developing equipment works."

Tomorrow. "Um, I can't come tomorrow."

Again the raised eyebrow. I saw my brand-new income circling the drain. "Why not? We're open Tuesday through Sunday."

"I'm so sorry." *Tell him the truth.* "I'll be going to church on Sundays. I—it's something new in my life that I haven't had to plan for before. But I do now." Not to mention I had a thirdterm paper to write on the economics of marriage in Jane Austen's *Emma* for English class on Tuesday.

He looked at me as if I said I was learning to rob convenience stores on Sundays. "A churchgoing woman," he said, "who can clean without complaint and make salsa on top of it. This is my lucky day."

I wasn't sure if he meant that or not. "Are you still going to hire me?" I hadn't even gotten a pen out of my bag to fill out the application yet. Talk about the world's shortest career.

"I've said I would. We'll each agree to keep our beliefs to ourselves, and we'll get along just fine. Your hours will be four until eight, Tuesday through Friday, with a half-hour dinner break at six. Saturdays ten till six. Will that suit?"

I'd keep Sundays, but I'd lose prayer circle. "Yes. That's perfect."

"Good." As we shook hands on the deal, I told myself I'd figure out how I was going to get my homework done. Maybe I could bring it along and do it behind the counter if business was slow. And maybe I could convince the girls to move prayer circle to eight-thirty on Tuesday nights instead of seven, without telling them why. Not even my friends needed to know why or how I was funding my dress.

As Gillian would say, I'd jump off that bridge when I got to it. The main thing was, I had myself a job.

LMansfield	Is Carly with you?
SHanna	No. I thought she was studying for the chem midterm with you guys.
LMansfield	Who's studying? Gillian went somewhere with Jeremy and I'm sitting here working on my Hearst essay and feeling sorry for myself.
SHanna	Poor baby. I have an invite to a gallery opening off Union Square. Some friend of my parents. There will be food. Want to come?
LMansfield	Meet you on the stairs in 15.

KEEPING A SECRET from your friends is harder than you'd think. Not because I was doing anything underhanded, but I was so happy about actually landing a job that I wanted to share it with them. Instead, I had to buckle my lips shut and look like I had nothing more important to think about than *Emma*.

On Sunday, when Bruno, the Mansfield family driver, came to get us and take us out to Marin for church and lunch with Lissa's folks, the news hovered on the tip of my tongue every time I opened my mouth.

But I couldn't spill.

Shani, who has gotten to know me pretty well since last term, gave me narrow-eyed looks all through the service and later, too, as we hung out on the deck behind the shambling redwood house on the hill after lunch. "What's up with you, girlfriend? You look different somehow."

I shrugged and kept my gaze on a hawk circling lazily over the oak trees. "Nothing. I probably gained five pounds over lunch. I knew I should have worn an empire-waisted dress."

She snorted, and Gillian and Lissa exchanged a look. "So where were you all day yesterday?"

"Shopping." It was the truth. I'd been in about ninety-five shops: drugstores, dress boutiques, eyewear stores, you name it. Nobody was hiring high-school kids. Except Sir Ian . . . whose real name turned out to be Philip Nolan.

My boss.

I practically hugged myself with glee.

"Shopping," Lissa repeated. "How come you didn't invite us along? If it hadn't been for Shani finally dragging me out, I'd have gone stir crazy, what with all my friends *deserting* me." Pointed glance at the rail, where Gillian lounged against a corner post and stared dreamily into space, completely oblivious to the, like, fifty-foot drop below her.

"I don't know." I thought fast. "It wasn't the fun kind." Which was true. "I didn't think you guys would be interested, so I just went." Time to get off the subject. "What I'd like to know is what Gillian was up to all day."

Bingo. Now three pointed glances swung in her direction.

"Yeah, Gillian," Shani said. "How was the big date with Jeremy?"

"It wasn't a date." Gillian tipped her head back, and a satisfied smile tilted up the corners of her mouth.

"I bet it was more than that." Lissa reached over and waggled Gillian's sandaled foot. "Look at that face, you guys. That's the face of a woman who's been kissed."

"Woot! Tell all," Shani said.

"What happens in Muir Woods stays in Muir Woods," Gillian informed us with maddening superiority.

"Aha! I was right." Lissa smiled wickedly. "But what I want to know is, is he a better kisser than Lucas Hayes?"

I hadn't heard that name mentioned in front of Gillian since last term. No big loss—for all his brilliance, the guy was a total loser, a liar, and a cheat. Someone told me that he'd gone to jail, but I'm sure that was only a rumor. Still, he'd given Gillian her first kiss, and she'd hung on to that memory like a souvenir of one beautiful moment on an otherwise horrible trip.

Gillian's satisfied smile widened. "Cone of silence?"

"Of course. You don't even need to ask," I said.

She swung both feet down and sat on the wide rail, facing us. "He'd kill me if he thought I'd told you guys, but scientific method has proven it. Jeremy is a *way* better kisser than Lucas."

"I love scientific method," Lissa said with faux dreaminess.

"Woo-hoo!" Hands high, Shani and I slapped palms in a victory salute.

"And he doesn't gawk at other girls, and he *never* tells me I talk too much."

"Mostly because you don't," I put in. "Only a guy who wanted all the attention for himself would think that."

I'd be happy if Brett noticed that I talked at all.

Evidently what had happened in Muir Woods wasn't going to stay there after all, because Gillian proceeded to tell us all about it, now that the headline news had broken. "So this means you guys are a couple," I said when she'd brought us all up to date. "Officially."

"I guess so." Gillian fiddled with her jade bead bracelet. "I mean, he hasn't said so in that many words, but we sit together in the dining room a lot, and his friends have stopped razzing him. Mostly. Which I think means they're getting used to the idea. Oh, and I've told my mom about him."

"Whoa." Shani looked impressed, then glanced at us. "I've met her mom. That *is* serious."

"Did she have a coronary?" I asked. "Was she afraid you'd flunk out and start doing drugs, just because you have a boyfriend?"

"No, my dad would think that," Gillian replied, rolling her eyes. "He has no clue. But you remember Jeremy came up from

Connecticut during break, and came to our house and met Mom and Nai-Nai then. Then he came up again to go to the musical with us, wearing his tux and everything. So it wasn't that big a stretch to ease her into thinking of him as my boyfriend, once she'd thought of him as Shani's and my friend from school."

"Good strategy." Lissa nodded in approval.

"She can break it to Dad. I'm not going to."

"Why do parents tweak out when we get a boyfriend?" Shani wanted to know. "Not that mine would be around long enough to notice. They went jetting off to Dubai this week, if you can believe it. What about you, Carly? What would your dad say?"

I snorted. "He's still in recovery about my mom having one. I don't think he could handle me, as well."

"That's different," Gillian said immediately. "Aren't they still married?"

I shook my head. "The divorce was final months ago. But that doesn't mean Dad doesn't still have feelings about it. I hear him . . ." My voice trailed away. I really didn't need to tell them about that. About the sounds I heard sometimes through the condo's walls late at night—my dad, talking to my mom as if she were still there. Sometimes he broke down, and I'd have to pull my pillow over my head to keep from eavesdropping on a moment so painfully private that no one should be allowed to listen.

"Anyway," I went on, "it's not like he has to worry about me."

Unfortunately.

chapter 8

TUESDAY MORNING, way before my alarm was set to go off, the tinny sound of electronic salsa music emanated from inside my book bag. It took me eight measures to wake up enough to realize what it was, and another four to find the cell phone.

Mac surfaced from under her quilt, swore viciously at me, and buried her head under her pillow.

Oops. Looked like we weren't going to be BFFs today, either.

"Hello?" I whispered.

"Hi, *poquita*."

I rolled onto my back in surprise. "Mama?"

"Who else?"

"What time is it?" I squinted at the clock.

A pause. "Uh-oh. Did I miscalculate the time difference again?"

"Uh, yeah, I think so. It's a quarter to six."

"Sorry, sweetie. I'm out by an hour. I was hoping to catch you before you started getting ready for classes."

"Well, you did."

She laughed, that bubbly, throw-your-head-back laugh that

was probably the thing I missed the most. That, and a real smile on my dad's face.

"I couldn't wait any longer. I thought about e-mailing you, or flying up to surprise you, and then I thought, oh, go ahead and call her."

"About what? What's happening?" I almost added, Are you coming home? Did you and Papa finally change your minds? But I didn't. That would be too good to be true. But why would she call all the way from Veracruz on my *abuelito's* phone card if it wasn't something huge?

"Well, remember the man you met when you were here on break? Richard Vigil?"

Duh. The guy with the salesman's smile and the leftover-eighties haircut. The guy who still thought narrow lapels and shoulder pads were in style. "Yes?" I said cautiously. Did I want to waste precious roaming minutes talking about him?

"Well, we went out to dinner on Sunday night at this little place on the harbor, and when my *dulce* came, you'll never guess what I found on it."

"A cockroach?"

Silence. "No, *mi'ja*. It wasn't that kind of restaurant."

"Oh, okay. I thought you might have gotten a free meal out of it, that's all. Go on."

"There were chocolate straws on my piece of cake, and a diamond ring was threaded onto one of them."

Now the silence was on my end. "What, did someone in the kitchen lose it?"

"No, *idiota*, it was Richard. He asked me to marry me, and I said yes!"

I lay still, staring at the plaster medallion in the ceiling where a chandelier had once hung, my eyes seeing it and my brain recording nothing. Just *I said yes, I said yes, I said yes* bouncing off the walls of my skull, echoing over and over.

"Carolina? *Poquita*, aren't you going to say anything?"

"Congratulations." Something was sitting on my chest. Something so heavy I could hardly draw the breath to say the word.

"Thank you, darling. I'm so excited. There are so many plans to make. We're going to be—"

"Have you told Papa?"

"—living in . . . Of course." Her tone changed. "Even though it doesn't really have anything to do with him, I called him as a courtesy. It's not the kind of thing you want to find out from other people."

"Or from your kids." I could just imagine poor Papa's face if I'd let something slip, thinking he knew. I didn't think I could have stood it.

"Anyway, Richard lives in Santa Fe, New Mexico, so I'll be moving back to the States as soon as we set a date. We'll be living in his house at first, but we'll start looking for a home of our own right away. And he's going to show my pieces in his gallery! Isn't that wonderful? You can come and live with us if you want, and get out of this ridiculous boarding school situation your father has you in."

Oh, no. I was not living within an entire state of Richard Vigil, and that was final. "I like this school."

"I'm sure you do, but you have to admit, it's not ideal."

"It's great. I'm learning a lot. And I've been invited to be on the committee that's organizing this huge fashion show. All the West Coast designers will be there. In fact, I was out with an oil-company heir and the daughter of an Italian princess just the other night, making plans for it."

The sound of long-distance buzzed. "Carolina, I'm not sure those are the kind of people you should be creating your future with. They're not real."

"If you pinch them, they yell, Mama. Would you rather I hung around with artistic types who are so busy living in the moment they can't handle a future at all?"

The second the words were out of my mouth, I wanted to take them back. I hadn't meant them to be about her, but I knew she'd take it that way.

"I'm going to forget I heard that," my mother said slowly. "I know this is a shock. I know you wanted your father and me to get back together. But that isn't real, either, Carolina."

"How realistic can it be to marry some guy you met on a cruise ship?"

"Richard has flown down here to see me three times since then," she informed me. "He has stayed under your *abuelito*'s roof and been a perfect gentleman. Your *abuelita* loves him. I want you to love him, too."

There was no reply I could possibly make to this, so this time I kept my mouth shut. Just as well. I needed to swallow the tears that swelled in my throat.

"And I want you and Alana to be my bridesmaids."

"What?"

"Of course. Who else? As soon as we have a wedding date and decide whether it's going to be in Veracruz or Santa Fe, I'll let you know. It will be such fun, choosing dresses and colors and things together."

I clamped my lips on the urge to ask her if she still had the dress she married Papa in. And the veil, and the something borrowed, something blue. "I don't want to, Mama."

A flood of chatter about Nile green versus salmon pink stopped in midstream. "*¿Qué?*"

"I'm not going to stand up with you. I don't like the guy, and I hate what you're doing to Papa."

"This has nothing to do with him."

"Yes, it does. This will kill him."

"Nonsense. Once he got over the surprise, he was delighted for me."

"He was lying, Mama. You know he'd never do anything to make you mad at him."

"Shows what you know. Even if he was, that's none of your business, Carolina. He's your father and you love him, and that's as it should be. But my life is my own now, and I choose to spend it with a man who worships me and who will support my art, not get in its way."

"Whatever. But I still don't want to be a bridesmaid."

I heard a hitch in her breath. "What's gotten into you, *poquita*? You never used to be so unkind."

I ignored the prickle in my conscience that told me the fruit of the Spirit—namely, love, joy, and peace—were withering on the vine here. But this *hurt*. I wanted to hit back at the thing that hurt me, like a little kid. "You and Papa never got divorced before. You never picked a guy in a turquoise shirt and a leather tie before."

The line clicked loudly in my ear. I threw my cell phone at the laundry basket.

How could she do this? How could she plow ahead, giggling and tossing her glossy long hair and pushing her ring into people's faces, while leaving the rest of the family miserable? Had my mother always been this self-centered? Was that what had made her leave us, not something we kids or my dad had done?

At that point I noticed Mac, leaning on one elbow and watching me. "That sounded interesting," she said. "Are you all right?"

"I'd rather not talk about it." I yanked my blankets over my head and burrowed deep under them, hoping they'd muffle the sounds of my misery as it rose up in a flash flood, sweeping away everything good I'd ever known.

⊠

To: alanaah@mac.com
From: caragon@spenceracad.edu
Date: April 21, 2009
Re: Mama

The future Mrs. Vigil called this morning to tell me the happy news. Are you going to be a bridesmaid? I'm not. This is horrible. I don't know how I'm going to face Papa.

I don't have anyone but you to talk to. Antony is too little. I'd never bring it up with Papa—it would wreck him. And I can't tell my friends—it wouldn't be right to blab family business to them, even if they're the best friends in the world.

Richard Vigil. I can't stand it. That hair! What does he do—watch his Duran Duran music videos in his spare time? How can our mother be this desperate?

Call me asap. I'm not available during class or between 4 and 8 pm but any other time is good.

Love, Carly

I hit Send and looked up as Mac came in. She dumped her backpack, which was army-surplus khaki and almost as beat-up as Gillian's, on the bed and pulled her laptop over without a word to me.

Which was fine. I was so not in the mood to make small talk when my family was being sucked into a black hole.

The way our room was set up, each of us could see the other while we were on our computers. Now, normally I'm all about keeping my head down and giving a person her privacy, but for some reason, while I was skimming my e-mail and trying to ignore her and all my other problems, I looked up.

Mac was checking e-mail too, but wow. Being a recent expert in bad news, I could tell when someone else was getting some. Her face was flushed, and she had that fragile look around the eyes that meant she was holding back tears.

She'd sworn at me this morning.

I'd shut her down.

Both of us were hurting, and I could do one of two things. I could leave her to it, and kiss good-bye any chance of finding a friend in her. Or I could swallow my pride and my fear of being flattened and reach out.

As Professor Dumbledore would say, sometimes you have to decide between what's right and what's easy.

"Is—is everything okay?"

She jumped and stared at me. "What's it to you?"

That was probably my cue to leave her to it, but that would have been too easy. "You look like you got e-mail as crappy as the phone call I got this morning."

Whatever blistering reply she'd been about to make about me minding my own business dissipated on a long breath. "Yeah, you could say so. Look, about this morning. I couldn't help but overhear."

"I'm sorry about that. My mother can never get the time difference right between here and Veracruz."

"Where?"

"It's a resort town on the Caribbean side of Mexico. She got engaged on the weekend."

"And you think it's pants?"

"If that's Scottish for *garbage*, then yeah. The guy is a relic from the eighties, and it's way too soon."

"For her or for you?"

I blinked. That was a weird way of putting it. "For her, of course." But that was dumb. Obviously it wasn't, or she wouldn't have sounded so bubbly and excited. And deluded, but that was just my opinion. "For me." With a sigh, I added, "Even though they're divorced, I guess I was hoping that someday she'd get back together with my father."

"Take it from me," Mac said. "The only person who hopes that is you. And you're the only person it hurts, too."

"Is this the voice of experience?"

She nodded. "My parents split up a couple of years ago. Mummy got the townhouse on Eaton Square, and Dad kept the ancestral pile in Scotland, of course. So I live with her and go to school in London and spend the hols with him at Strathcairn."

"Do you like it?"

With a lift of one shoulder, she said, "I live with it. She lunches with the ladies who still introduce her as the Countess, and Dad lets tour groups come through and gawk while he hides in the cellar, experimenting with terrible batches of whiskey. The only reason he could pay the taxes last year was because of your friend Lissa's dad. They gave him a small fortune to use the place as a location for that movie."

"I thought you were rolling in it." I glanced at her closet. "You wear Chanel."

"Mummy is rolling in it," Mac said dryly. "It's the classic setup—he's got the title, she's got the dosh. The perfect marriage. Only . . ." Her voice trailed away for a moment. "I think they really were happy. You know. Before. I just can't get either of them to tell me what happened."

"Neither can I. We had such a great life. Everyone always laughing, lots of family around. Tons of food, women yakking in the kitchen, telling stories about the men behind their backs. I learned more about life in Mama's kitchen than in any sex ed class. And then it all just"—I waved my hands, *abracadabra*— "disappeared." Mac nodded as if she could relate. "So when she called to say she was engaged and would I be her bridesmaid, all that played into it. I guess I was mean to her, but I couldn't help it."

"Understandable. She needs to give you a little time."

"Knowing my mother, both of them will turn up here tomorrow to smooth things over."

"I hope not."

"Me, too." I looked up. "So. Enough about me. What lovely piece of news did you get?"

She looked at her screen as if she'd managed to forget about it for five minutes. I was almost sorry I'd asked. "No news. Just . . . it's odd."

"What is?"

She turned the laptop in my direction. "What do you make of this?"

....

✉

To: lmacphail@spenceracad.edu
From: drifter1989@gmail.com
Date: April 20, 2009
Re: Found you

The beauty of the Net is that people are so easy to find. How come you didn't tell me you were going to the States, Linds? If my friend hadn't told me, I'd never have known you'd jetted off to San Francisco.

I wasn't expecting the heat. And it's not exactly England's green and pleasant land, is it? I thought this place would be more glamorous, like in *The O.C.* Instead it just looks dry. How come you came here for your exchange term? I called and they told me you were doing that. Something else I had to find out from a stranger. I wish you'd write to me. I love you.

Anyway, I thought you'd like this for a souvenir. Or maybe the press will.

You know. After.
Drifter

....

Attached was an image file. When I clicked on it, the image filled the screen and I sucked in a breath. It was a picture of the two of us, half-turned away from the camera, an orange cab in the background. I wore a blue silk jacket and Mac wore her Prada dress. I looked up into Mac's face. Her lips were pressed together, as if she was trying to keep them from trembling.

"This is from the night we went to TouTou's," I said. I wasn't about to forget that dress, or how I'd felt coming second to her in it. "How did he get this? Who is this Drifter guy?" I studied the picture again. "Your boyfriend? Or, um, ex?"

"No!" She snatched the laptop away and closed it, as if something bad might jump out of the screen. "I don't even know the silly nit. I delete his messages, but he just keeps on."

I'd seen her deleting things, stabbing at them angrily, as if that would make them go away faster—or more permanently. "He seems to think he knows you, though. He must be one of the photographers that hang around here." I tried to remember, but the events later had blanked out trivial things, like people taking pictures.

"He's been sending me mail for months. I hate it. I wish he would stop. Or better yet, step in front of a train." She looked close to tears.

She didn't even know this person, and yet he'd said he loved her. That was weird. And scary. And there was a name for it.

"Along with Chanel Couture and the Balenciagas," I said slowly, "it looks like you've got a stalker."

chapter 9

"YOU MUSTN'T TELL ANYONE."

Why do people say stuff like this? Why does the girl in the horror movie always go down to the basement after she hears the window break? Or wait to call the police until *after* the bad guy is in the house?

"Mac, you can't just let him do this to you. You have to report it. At least tell Ms. Curzon."

"What's she going to do?"

"I don't know. But there's a no-harassment rule here. The first thing they'd probably do is change your e-mail addy."

"I never gave him the first one." She stared at the sleeping laptop. "I've never even answered any of his messages."

"But Curzon will tell the cops to go after his provider. They'll give out his address and he'll be arrested. End of stalk."

"I doubt that. He hasn't actually done anything to be arrested for."

"How'd he get this picture? He's hanging around here. There must be something they can pick him up for."

Even though it was a warm afternoon in late April, Mac got up and shut the window. Maybe it made her feel safer. "It's weird. But I mean what I say, Carly. This is off the grid."

"Why? I don't get you."

"There will be a huge noise about it. And the tabs will print it, and whoever this guy is will know he's freaked me out. He'll probably get off on it, the sniveling numpty."

Part of me admired her vocab while the rest of me just felt exasperated. "Or," I said reasonably, "Ms. Curzon will do a confidential investigation, they'll pull the guy's plug, and off he'll go to court or whatever, with no one the wiser."

"Carly, it doesn't work that way. I can't even color my hair without some British tab shrieking about how awful it looks."

"We're not in Britain. All the tabs here care about is who Vanessa is wearing this week."

"Yes, but all the paparazzi know each other. There are stringers for the British papers out front right now. How else does Vanessa get into *Hello!*?"

"Uh, she pays someone?"

Mac slanted a look at me. "Very funny. But you hear what I'm saying. He could be out front pretending to be one of them right now."

"I don't think ignoring him is the right thing to do."

"And I think it is."

From the set of her mouth and the expression in her eyes, which was going from miserable to combative, I caved. "At the very least, print every message you get from him before you delete them, okay? And keep them somewhere. At least then we'll have hard evidence if we need it."

I sounded like Gillian, who owns possibly every *CSI* episode ever aired, plus bonus footage. But maybe sounding like her wasn't a bad thing.

Mac nodded and hit Print, and with relief I pulled it off the wireless printer we shared in its cubbyhole under my desk. "You deleted all the other ones?"

"Of course. I couldn't stand to look at them. He never says anything bad. They're mostly kind of pathetic. But they made me angry and scared and it felt good to just wipe them out of existence."

"Well, don't wipe any more, okay? We might need them."

"I've said I would, and I will. And what's this *we* business?" I stared at her, confused. We? Wii? *Oui*? "This is not your problem. You are not involved."

I tried not to feel hurt. "I got involved when he took my picture with you. Try to think, Mac. It must be someone you know. How else would they know about you coming here?"

"Carly, didn't you hear me?"

"I can't hear you when you sound like my mother."

"Don't get your knickers in a twist. I only meant that it could be dangerous. I don't want any of this to hurt you."

"But it's okay if something happens to you?"

"It's my problem. I'll deal."

I thought of Lissa braving the Benefactors' Day Ball and getting out there under that spotlight, despite the giggles and murmurs I could hear in the audience. And of Gillian, facing down her abusive ex-boyfriend in the school cafeteria and inciting a food fight.

People didn't have to solve everything alone. They could ask for help. And if they couldn't or didn't know they could ask God for it, there was always the second option.

Us.

"You don't have to deal alone," I said. "Fine, you can keep it to yourself if you want. But I'm here if you need me."

She looked down her aristocratic nose. Her gaze measured me from head to foot. I braced myself for another crushing put-down.

And then her eyes filled with tears.

But it was like she was frozen in her seat. As if getting up and taking one step toward me would make her crack and all her feelings would come oozing out.

Before she could take a breath to say a word, I crossed the room and bent down to where she sat in front of her laptop. I gave her a hug.

"You are the nicest person I've ever met," she choked, and began to cry for real.

....

✉

To: lmacphail@spenceracad.edu
From: strathcairn2@bt.co.uk
Date: April 23, 2009
Re: Settling in?

Hello darling. I hope everything is going well for you at this new school. I knew Natalie Curzon when we were children; it seems strange to think you and she are in the same place now, so far away. I've never been farther west than New York.

All is much the same here. I saw Lily Allen at a movie premiere and she wanted me to remind you that you promised her a weekend in L.A. I've no idea what that's about, but there you are. Saw Wills and Kate and Harry at the Goldsmiths' Hall and they send their regards.

Everyone misses you, darling, me most of all. Have you heard from your father recently?

Love, Mummy

....

"DON'T FORGET—prayer circle tonight." Gillian paused on the wide second-floor landing and let her fifty-pound backpack slide down to rest on her instep. If she ever got mugged, she could use the thing for a lethal weapon. "You're coming, right?"

I opened my mouth to say yes and then remembered. "I—I can't. I have something else I need to do."

I tried not to squirm under that dark-eyed gaze. "But you always come. And fellowship is important. What have you got going? Extracurriculars? Or wait." She held up a palm. "The committee's having a meeting."

I shook my head. "Nothing like that." I turned to go up the next flight of stairs. "See you tomorrow." I'd already run up half a dozen when she said, totally confused, "But, Carly . . ."

How to feel completely lame in one easy lesson.

Gillian deserved a better reason than that. And it wasn't like I didn't want to go. I did. There was something about praying out loud with my friends that made me feel . . . I don't know. Safe. Deeper. More solid. It's hard to explain.

But I had to go to work, and I'd already missed the three-fifteen bus.

I threw on a pair of cargo pants and a T-shirt, then popped on a Marc Jacobs linen jacket over it. I took a couple of extra minutes to dash down the first-floor corridor to the dining room and snag a sandwich and a bottle of Odwalla strawberry lemonade from the refrigerator case. It would be warm by the time I got my dinner break, but there wasn't much I could do about that. Then, stuffing them into my tote bag, which already held my math homework, I pelted across the field and made the three-thirty bus with seconds to spare.

Luckily, I was used to hiking up and down the steep streets around here. I was hardly even breathing fast as the bus pulled away from the curb and headed downtown. It dropped me on the opposite side of the street from Piccadilly Photo, and I was in the back of the shop pulling on my lab coat by five minutes to four.

Philip finished writing up what looked like thirty rolls of someone's vacation pictures and walked the lady to the front door.

"Doesn't she know about digital cameras?" I gathered all the rolls up in a wire tray and got them into the development queue. All my pictures were online so I could share them with my family.

I'd already washed and waxed the floors over the course of a couple of days last week, so today's task was to polish all the display cabinets—again—and find a way to jazz up the displays of Nikons and Canons and their lenses. After that, Philip had promised to teach me how the developer worked. It was kind of intimidating to me, but once I knew how to develop pictures myself, he could take a break once in a while and leave me to run the shop on my own.

"I'm glad she doesn't. The cameras may pay the rent, but I do like a bit of jam with my bread and butter." By which, I gathered, he meant that he liked the income from the photo development, too. "Have you thought of any ways to make all this hardware more visually appealing?"

"If you're in the market for a camera, it's pretty appealing already."

"Most people, Carly, don't know they're in the market for a camera. They have to be reminded. Hence my question."

Not even Mr. Milsom, terror of the science labs, used a word like *hence*. Only one of the reasons I thought my boss was either a few cards short of a full deck, or one of the coolest old guys I'd ever met. I couldn't decide which.

I got out the Windex and a pile of clean rags. "My father says that ninety percent of marketing is making someone want what they don't need."

"A man of sense."

"He is. I don't know what my mother was thinking." I stopped myself and got back on topic. "So what we should do maybe is not show people the actual stuff as much as what they'll get when they have it. You know. Benefits instead of features."

"Which are?"

I scrubbed at a stubborn nose print until the glass squeaked. Ew. People should wipe off their kids before they brought them in here. "Well, where do people have good times? At a wedding. Or a holiday. Like that lady who just left. Show people having fun with their cameras."

"Make it part of their experience. Hmm." Philip's face took on a faraway expression. "We could blow up some good shots and display them with the equipment that produced them."

"You could have workshops on how to get pictures like that. Do them online, even. This place has a Web site, right?"

"Er, no."

"Philip, Philip." I shook my head with mock despair and gave him a smile. "How am I going to drag you into the twenty-first century?"

"With as little pain as possible, I hope. You must allow I'm getting there at my own pace, snail-like though it may be."

"The point is, there are lots of ways to get people involved with their cameras, which means they're involved with Piccadilly Photo, right?"

"Right. How have I stayed in business this long without you?"

I grinned at him. "It's a mystery."

He was silent for so long, I figured he was planning out his marketing campaign. I'd actually finished polishing up the longest display case, which ran down the side of the shop, when he spoke again.

"What was that you said about your mother?"

I stopped. "Huh?" My arm ached, so I switched the rag to the other hand.

"You said something about your dad having sense, but you didn't know what your mother was thinking. What was that about?"

I ducked down and began at the bottom of the next case. "Nothing."

"I think it is something."

"It's a long story."

"We have a long evening ahead of us. Punctuated, one hopes, by the arrival of customers."

I sighed. "Philip, you can't possibly be interested in my boring problems or my boring family."

"Since the latter managed to produce a fine young woman despite what you say, I think I'm very interested. Provided you want to tell me. You can always just ask me to mind my own business."

I'd never been very good about keeping things to myself. I'd always had someone around to talk things over with—Papa, my mother, Alana. Even now I talked to Shani more than anyone—just not about family business. But Philip was different. He was an adult. He'd been around. And best of all, he was completely separate from the rest of my life.

So I told him. About the divorce, about us kids living in three different cities, about our family going from one big happy Mexican-American hive to all these rootless little satellites, their orbits intersecting only once in a while.

"And now my mom tells me she's engaged to this doofus who lives in Santa Fe, New Mexico. He put a diamond ring in her dessert last weekend. Be still, my heart. She wants me and my sister, Alana, to be her bridesmaids."

"And will you?" Philip took a rag and squirted Windex on the other side of the cabinet I was working on.

"Are you kidding? The last thing I want to do is stand there in a big poofy dress, watching her vow to love, honor, and cherish. She didn't do that for my father, did she?"

"Maybe she did, in the beginning."

"Yeah, well, there's more to a marriage than the beginning. There's the middle, too."

"That is the hard part."

"My dad isn't hard to live with. He's never there, for one thing."

"Which may have contributed to the problem."

Both of us were crouched down, looking at each other over the Canons as we polished the panels of glass. "What do you mean?"

"It's difficult to love, honor, and cherish someone who isn't there."

"They could talk on the phone. Or IM or something."

"People do grow apart. Maybe that's what happened."

I caught my reflection in a metal strip and tried to smooth out the grumpy frown lines in my forehead. "How can you know that?"

"I don't, of course. But possibly you don't know the whole story, either. I'd want to shield my children from as much as possible, if it were me."

I looked up. "Do you have kids?"

"One son. He's a teacher in Vermont."

"And your wife?"

"Gone."

"Gone how?"

I'd meant divorced, left, whatever, but he said simply, "In the usual way. She passed in 1985, when Kimball was still a child."

The smell of ammonia went up my nose. I realized my hand was pressed to my mouth, as if it were preventing one more whiny, complaining word from coming out of it. "Oh, Philip. I'm so sorry."

"I am, too."

"I didn't mean to go on about my dumb stuff when you've had worse things happen."

He lifted a shoulder. "I wanted to hear about your 'stuff.' You might think about doing this thing for your mother, Carly. I can tell you from experience that chances to do things for each other can be taken away, just like that. And then you spend the rest of your life wishing you'd had just a few more minutes." He stared through the glass at the Sony videocam on its pedestal, without seeming to see it. "Just to say yes. Or to bring them a glass of cold water. Or to give them a kiss to say you love them." He looked up, and I had no doubt that he saw me in every glaring detail. "Or to catch a bouquet that they threw just for you."

chapter 10

S O MUCH FOR professional distance.

As I rode back to school on the eight-twenty bus, I regretted telling Philip all the stuff I had. After all, when you tell somebody something, it isn't to hear what you already know. It's to get a different perspective, right? Or find a different way of solving the problem.

Going to the wedding and doing what my mom wanted was, in Philip's mind, the right thing to do. But it just seemed wrong to me, when she'd never done anything us kids had ever wanted. Nobody had asked us when she'd left, had they? Nobody wanted our opinion about her going back to her parents in Veracruz—who, incidentally, lived in a beautiful house my dad had paid for. He'd done that out of love for her, and what had she done for him?

I got off the bus and crossed the playing field as the last of the sunset faded to purple over the skyline and lights began to wink on all over the city.

I should have been paying more attention. That's what they tell you in self-defense classes: "Be aware of your surroundings."

If I hadn't been so deep in my own thoughts, I'd have had a few seconds to prepare myself when a shape wearing a hoodie loomed up on my right.

"Hey, Carly," Brett Loyola said.

My heart seized up and I froze.

"It's just me," he said. "Brett. Sorry, I didn't mean to scare you."

Scare me? Two of my dreams had just come true, right there in the middle of the plushy grass field. One, Brett Loyola had remembered my name, and two, he'd spoken to me of his own volition, without chemistry notes or his entourage around him. What was he doing without Callum or Todd or one of the innumerable girls who always followed them around?

"Carly? You okay?" He leaned in to try to see my face.

"Yes," I squeaked, then cleared my throat and tried again. "Sure. I didn't realize anyone was there, that's all."

"You did look kind of preoccupied, all right. Mind if I walk with you?"

Mind? Was he crazy? This was probably a hallucination or a dream, but I was going to enjoy it for all it was worth.

"No, not at all. Are you heading back to school?" I asked. "Aren't you a day student?"

"Yeah, I am, but some of the guys are going out, so I said I'd meet them in the common room."

Oh. "Sounds like fun."

"Want to come with us?"

"I'd be taking my life in my hands," I said, trying for a joke to give myself a second to recover.

"Nah. We're just going downtown to hang out, maybe have a drink. I want to apologize, by the way."

My mind went blank. To the best of my knowledge, we hadn't been together enough for him to be sorry for anything. "Why?"

"The other night, when I ordered that drink for you without asking what you wanted. That was pretty ignorant."

"You were being thoughtful."

"By getting you a Cosmo when you don't drink? I don't think so."

A glow began to spread all over me. Yep, definitely a dream. I'd fallen asleep on the bus and had probably ridden all the way downtown to the terminus, but I didn't care. *Please, nobody wake me up.*

"Well, thanks for the apology, anyway, even if it wasn't necessary."

We'd nearly reached the trees at the side of the main building. If this was a dream, surely I should be able to say something witty and brilliant, something I'd never say in real life. Something daring that would get his attention, once and for all.

"So Vanessa says you're a Christian." I couldn't really be sure in the dark under the trees, but I thought he'd turned his head to look at me as we walked. "And that's why you didn't want it."

Was that good or bad in his mind? "Yes," I said a little cautiously. "I'm kind of a noob though."

"A newbie Christian?" He chuckled, as if that was an odd concept.

"I mean, I just made the decision really recently. I don't know very much yet."

"What's to know?"

"That's the thing. I don't even know that. How much there is to know, I mean. I'm kind of feeling my way along, and my friends are helping me a lot. My family is Catholic, so at least I learned something when I was a kid."

"Yeah, mine, too. But I stopped going to mass a long time ago. Saturday nights aren't exactly conducive to matins or whatever the next morning, you know?"

I laughed because he did, and because here was proof this had to be a dream. There was no way I'd be talking about my faith with Brett Loyola in real life. No way.

"Gillian organized the prayer circle, and she and Lissa talk with me about whatever I want to know," I went on. "We go to church together on Sundays."

"I came to that prayer circle thing once," he said. "Kinda bizarre."

"It got better," I said quickly. I remembered that night. Boy, did I. "A bunch of kids come now. There was one tonight, in fact."

"Is that where you were?"

"No, I was"—I stopped myself just in time—"out."

"Skiving off, huh?" In the lights from the front windows, I could see he was smiling at me.

"Oh, no. I just had something I had to do tonight." I paused. "What does that mean? Skiving off?"

His grin widened. "That's something your roomie taught me. It means skipping out. Cutting."

The glow from the lights flattened into a glare as I hurried up the front steps. With his long stride, though, he beat me to the door and opened it for me.

"Thank you." We walked into the main entry hall together.

"Anytime. Nice talking to you." He paused in the doorway to the common room. "Let Lindsay know we're meeting in here, okay?" he added. "She said she might come."

"Oh?" I hardly knew what I was saying. I was too busy waking up from the dream and realizing it was a nightmare. "She did?"

"Sure you won't change your mind?"

I smiled vaguely at him. "I have about eight hours of homework ahead of me." Which was the truth. And it shows you just how uncool I was. What woman in her right mind would do homework instead of going downtown with Brett Loyola, especially when he'd asked her twice in the space of five minutes?

I'll tell you who was in her right mind.

Lady Lindsay MacPhail.

◦◦◦

EOverton	You will never ever guess who just came in with BL.
DGeary	Vanessa? Are they back together?
EOverton	No.
DGeary	Tell.
EOverton	MexiDog.
DGeary	!!!!!!!! Came in like they happened to be at the door together, or came in like they WERE together?
EOverton	Door number 2. As in, holding it for her and everything.
DGeary	OMG. What is he thinking? I thought he was hot for Her Highness.
EOverton	The man likes to slum, as we know too well.
DGeary	Well, yeah, but this is going a little far. Does VT know?
EOverton	I'm not gonna be the one to tell her.
DGeary	You got that right.

◦◦◦

MAC LAY ON HER BED, intent on her laptop. She glanced up as I came in. "You had your phone turned off."

That was one of the first things Philip had made crystal-clear. No personal calls during work hours. "I know. Were you trying to call me?"

"Not me. Lissa and Gillian both called on the room phone around seven, as did a person called Alana."

"That's my sister. She lives in Texas. She does sound design for a recording studio in Austin."

"Does she?" Mac looked interested. "Do you ever notice the number of things that need to be designed? Sound design. Hair design. Interior design. What is with that?"

I was so not interested in a philosophical discussion of semantics when I was still trying to recover from massive disappointment. "Brett says to tell you that they're meeting in the common room, if you want to join them."

She pushed the laptop away. "Oh. Is that tonight?"

"I guess." I took my math textbook out of my bag and tried to calculate how many of the assigned exercises I could get through before dawn.

"Do you mind?"

What had we been talking about? "Mind what?"

"Mind that Brett asked me to go with them."

"Why should I? He asked me, too."

"Did he?" She smiled and pushed up the pillow behind her back, as if she were settling in for a girl-to-girl talk. "And of course you said yes."

"No, I didn't." I glanced up. "Look, if you're going to go, you should. I have about five tons of homework to do."

"You turned down Brett Loyola to do homework?"

Basically what I'd been asking myself—and kicking myself over—all the way upstairs. "Don't rub it in."

"Why didn't you do your homework earlier? You really need to learn some time management skills."

Okay, that did it. My emotions had been batted all over the place today, and I did not need this. "There's nothing wrong with my time management skills. I had something to do this afternoon, all right? And it took until eight. Why is everybody giving me such a hard time about it?"

She gazed at me for a few seconds. "You do mind."

"I told you, I don't. All I'm trying to do is get a dress into this fashion show and everyone is giving me grief about it." Okay, so I'd left out a couple steps—like getting a job so I could get some fabric—but my lips had to stay sealed about that part. Especially with Mac. I still wasn't a hundred percent sure she'd understand what being a scholarship kid meant, and why I had to keep it under the radar.

She opened her mouth to say something else, but her laptop pinged to announce a new e-mail message. When she glanced down at the screen, the color drained from her face.

"Mac." My irritation seeped away, too. "What's wrong?"

She lifted her gaze to mine as if it took a lot of effort. "It's him."

I dropped my math book and sat on the bed next to her, all thoughts of Brett and my impossible social life evaporating. There in the colorful list of her e-mail was a new message from Drifter. "Are you going to open it?"

"I'm afraid to."

It was hard for me to imagine her being afraid of anyone. Vanessa Talbot was about the scariest thing I'd ever met, and Mac had faced her down without even breaking a nail.

"Go on," I said. "Maybe he'll let something slip that will help us figure out who he is."

....

✉

To: lmacphail@spenceracad.edu
From: drifter1989@gmail.com
Date: April 28, 2009
Re: California girls

I heard the Beach Boys playing in the café tonight and had to laugh. I wish they all could be, etc. Do you think of yourself as a California girl now? Never mind. The point is, you're here and I'm here and soon everyone will . . . but I can't tell.

Drifter
....

"Soon everyone will what?" I asked.

Mac just shook her head, staring at the e-mail as though it might refresh itself and offer a clue.

"Why is he so creepy? Is he trying to scare you?"

"I don't know what he's thinking." At least anger was beginning to beat back the fear in her voice. "I don't know why he's picked me to vent on. Or how he found me in the first place."

"How long did you say he's been writing to you?"

She shrugged. "Months."

"I can't believe you haven't told anyone."

"Told them what? The first messages were just chatty little one-liners. I thought it was one of my mates from school, but I soon found out it wasn't. Then I thought maybe it was some weirdo off MySpace, so I took down my page." She glanced at me and pressed Print, and in a second the wireless laser printer spat out the e-mail. "I don't answer them, but they don't stop coming. They just get longer and more pathetic. With pictures. And now they're in my school mailbox, which only my parents and Carrie have."

"Could it be someone Carrie knows?"

"We know all the same people. If she knew, I'd know. And I don't even remember seeing anyone the night he took that picture. Look, we've been over all this before and we're no further ahead. I'm sick of it." She shut the laptop down and slid it into her bag.

"Okay. So. Are you going to go with Brett and those guys?" Not the best topic to switch to, but I couldn't think of anything else.

She shrugged. "I may as well. And leave you with your prep."

I did the mental translation: homework. "Thanks."

She changed out of her uniform into a pair of jeans, with a tank and a silk babydoll top over it that tied in the back with a black silk ribbon.

"That's adorable," I said. "Where'd you get it?"

"London. Topshop, I think. Do you suppose Brett will notice?"

"He's a guy." I hoped my attempt at sarcasm hid the sinking feeling in my middle. "Of course he will."

I thought that might cheer her up a little, but she didn't smile. She just grabbed an equally adorable Mulberry handbag and flitted out of the room as if she'd completely forgotten her fright over the e-mail, leaving me with fifty word problems and an urge to seek and consume the biggest chocolate bar in the vending machine.

DGeary	Did you hear the news?
CPowell	Chris Brown is playing the Fillmore?
DGeary	I wish. Try again.
CPowell	Vanessa and Brett are back together?
DGeary	No. But close.
CPowell	I give up. I'm losing neurons over these word problems. Come save me.
DGeary	I just heard that Brett went out with Carly Aragon.
CPowell	Who??
DGeary	aka MexiDog.
CPowell	OMG. Are you sure?
DGeary	Got it straight from an eyewitness. And, no, VT does not know.
CPowell	Isn't she the one rooming with Lady L?
DGeary	The same.
CPowell	Wow. Who is she?
DGeary	Up until now I'd have said nobody. Some people think he's slumming. But now I'm not so sure.
CPowell	Maybe we should invite her to your party Friday.
DGeary	Ya think?

chapter 11

N EXT TO VANESSA, probably the most scarifying
person at Spencer is Ms. Curzon, the headmistress.
So naturally, guess who stopped me in the corridor the
next day on my way to fifth-period Spanish.

"I was hoping I might run into you," she said with a smile.

I flipped through the last couple of days at top speed. What
had I done wrong? Were students here supposed to tell the administration when they got jobs?

"Really?" I said faintly when I came up with nothing.

"I wondered how you were managing now that you're sharing
a room."

I pasted on a smile as bright as hers had been. "Fine."

"I'm glad to hear it. Unfortunately, the news about Lady Lindsay's identity got out a little sooner than I would have liked."

"She asked me not to call her that. I call her Mac."

"Did she? I'm afraid I have no choice. 'Miss MacPhail' simply
isn't correct, though I would have continued to use it if we'd
managed to keep our secret."

I wondered what all this had to do with me. I glanced down

the corridor to the door of my Spanish classroom. It hadn't closed yet, which meant I wasn't late.

She followed my glance. "I won't keep you. But I did want to ask if everything was working out for the two of you. Lady Lindsay did, after all, request a change of room at the beginning of term."

"It's fine," I said again. "We've . . . begun to get along." The urge to tell her about Mac's e-mail stalker welled up, and I struggled to squash it down. Not my decision. Mac had told me to keep it quiet. If I blabbed about it to the headmistress, Mac would never forgive me for breaking her confidence.

But what if breaking a confidence was the right thing to do? How was a person supposed to know? Was this the kind of thing Gillian and Lissa would talk to God about? Could you talk to God in front of someone?

Lord? Lord, what should I do?

"I knew you were the right choice to share with her," Ms. Curzon said. "You're a down-to-earth, sensible girl. You can be a good influence on her."

I doubt that. Then I realized with horror I'd actually said it out loud.

"I realize you've had very different upbringings. But she's a long way from home and could use a friend."

Lots of the students here were a long way from home. Gillian, for one. And the principal wasn't going around looking for friends for her.

I just smiled.

"Thank you, Miss Aragon." She patted me on the arm. "Off you go, now. I see that Señorita de la Cruz is waiting at the door."

At least I didn't get a demerit for being late. I slid into my seat and tried to figure out what that had all been about.

"If you ask me," Shani said the next morning as we ate breakfast together, "she just wants to keep the hush money."

"Hush money? What?" I stirred fruit into my bowl of yogurt. Shani, always doing her own thing, sprinkled sugar and raisins on her oatmeal. Lissa has turned the Spencer breakfast staple into a standing joke, but I think Shani actually likes it.

"Well, maybe not hush money, but you've got to believe having Mac here will only raise Spencer's profile. Think of the new enrollments. I mean, the spawn of computer moguls and local money is one thing. But titled Scottish heiresses are another kettle of haggis—as dear Vanessa will be the first to tell you, since she snagged her to head up the fashion show."

"What is haggis, and what is it doing in a kettle?"

She told me, and I wished I hadn't asked. "Maybe Curzon was honestly concerned. I mean, you've got to admit the girl is intimidating."

"Who's intimidating?"

My stomach flip-flopped and sank as Mac put her plate of *huevos rancheros* on the table next to me and slid into a chair.

"You." Shani smiled with so much charm that one of those cartoon sparkles practically glinted off her teeth.

I kicked her under the table.

"Rubbish." Mac poked at her eggs. "What on earth is this?"

Maybe *huevos* were to her what haggis was to me. I told her and she took an experimental bite.

"No *huevos* in Scotland?" Shani asked, minus the charm and more like the real girl who was my friend.

"Not like this, with the spicy bits," Mac said, taking another bite. "This is good."

"Remind me to take you to my favorite place south of San Jose," I said. Not that I thought she'd ever take me up on it. "They make the best *chiles rellenos* ever. And their green chile *enchiladas* are to die for."

"Don't you go home every weekend?" she asked.

I started to nod, then stopped. I had to work on Saturdays. I might have been able to get away with staying in San Francisco last weekend because Papa was out of the country, but it couldn't go on forever. In fact, I needed to tell him what I was doing. Would Enrique still be willing to come and get me on Saturday nights after eight? Or would Papa finally quit being all protective and macho and admit that I was old enough to do something as simple as hop on BART and take a train down to the South Bay?

"Her dad sends a limo every Friday, like clockwork." I hoped Shani didn't think that would impress a girl like Mac, who probably had a fleet of limos on permanent retainer.

"Maybe he wouldn't mind if I joined you sometime, then." Mac paused when I didn't reply. I couldn't. I was stunned into speechlessness. "Do you ever have people stay with you?"

"Um . . . not usually," I managed. Then, in case she thought I was brushing her off, I added, "I have a little brother, and half the time a bunch of semi-cousins are over, all his age. I wouldn't want to inflict that kind of pain on any of my friends."

I met her eyes and smiled, and for the first time she smiled back—not a social smile or a condescending one or the deceptive kind Vanessa uses to get what she wants. A real one. The kind friends share over an inside joke or a memory.

"I'd be willing to risk it," she said. "I'd like to see where you live."

"Me, too," Shani put in. "How about it, Carly? Some of us could stand to get away from here once in a while."

"Um . . ." I tried to think of some reason why they couldn't come spend a weekend with me—other than the real ones, of course. There weren't enough bedrooms. We only lived in a condo. Papa had so little time with us that the weekends together as a family were precious.

Papa. That was it.

"My father's out of town a lot," I mumbled. "It's hard to schedule a time when he's there so he can meet you all."

"Not that I wouldn't love to meet your dad," Mac said, scooping up the last of the *papitas* on her plate, "but we could have a good time without him, too, yeah?"

"Well, when he's gone we stay with my sort-of aunt and the previously mentioned horde of semi-cousins."

"You don't stay on your own?" Mac looked surprised. "When Mum goes off for the weekend, she always lets me have the flat to myself. I have one or two mates over, and we have a great time."

"No," I had to confess. "Papa is old-fashioned." It would never occur to him to leave the two of us alone, without family or Tía Donna there. Not that I couldn't cook up a big batch of Antony's favorite *carnitas* and look after us myself, but Papa wouldn't hear of it.

"Her dad loves her," Shani said loyally. "When she comes home, he wants to be there. I think that's great."

I gave her a big smile. Shani's a little scary before you get to know her, but once she lets you in, she's rock solid.

"Are you insinuating," Mac said coolly, "that my mum doesn't love me? That she abandons me?"

Shani looked blank. "Of course not. I'm the last person to say that."

"Oh?"

"Yeah. Ever wonder why I'm in boarding school?"

"No, I hadn't given it much thought."

"It's so my parents don't have to be bothered with me. And I like that just fine." She glanced at me. "I think Carly's lucky. Somebody cares about where she is. And about being there when she is."

Well, somebody might if they knew. Guilt prickled through me. I really, really needed to have a conversation with Papa, and soon. Although how I was going to explain how I needed a job more than I needed to see my family, I wasn't sure.

CPowell	Are you busy after dinner?
GChang	What's up?
CPowell	I need serious help with these word problems. Do you tutor?
GChang	I would if I had time, but I'm pretty crazed right now. Try Travis Fanshaw.
CPowell	Thanks. Aren't you friends with Carly Aragon?
GChang	Yes.
CPowell	Do you have her cell number? Emily and DeLayne are having a party at Callum McCloud's place and I want to invite her.
GChang	??
CPowell	It's only polite. Brett's coming. Vanessa doesn't know.
GChang	Again, ??
CPowell	You must not be very good friends then. Her number?
GChang	408-555-0710.
CPowell	Tx. I'll call Travis, too.
GChang	What's going on?
GChang	Hello?

THAT EVENING, I got my first paycheck. Hustling into the office at the back of Piccadilly Photo where Philip places his orders and does owner stuff, I ripped open the envelope.

Two hundred and eighty dollars? For two weeks' hard work?

I smacked myself on the forehead. How could I have forgotten about income tax and all that stuff that comes out of your check before you see it? Stifling a groan, I pulled out Philip's chair and sank into it.

I could buy a grand total of two yards of fabric. Or half of one shoe. There were six weeks of school left. Even if I had two more paychecks, there wouldn't be time to order fabric from England or Italy, never mind make a dress. I still hadn't come up with the most important thing—a design.

I tried to calm down and slow my heart rate. What I needed to do was fall back to Plan B.

Just as soon as I came up with it.

The bell over the door rang a couple times in succession, so I stuffed the check in the pocket of my lab coat and went out to the front. As I took in rolls of film for a guy in his twenties, I tried to be polite and businesslike while my brain galloped like a hamster on a wheel.

Fabric. Time. Homework. Work. Brett. Fabric, time, homework, work, Brett. FabrictimehomeworkworkBrett.

I blinked and realized the guy had left and I was now helping a lady choose a digital camera. I'd somehow lost twenty minutes.

Any more of this and I'd be losing my mind.

At eight I said good night to Philip and got on the bus. I turned my phone on and nearly jumped out of my seat when it rang a couple of seconds later.

"Hi Carly, this is Christine Powell."

It took me a second to place her. Oh, yeah. She hung around with DeLayne Geary, in Vanessa's second tier of friends. "Hi. How's it going?"

She moaned. "These word problems. I'm dying, I swear."

Surely she couldn't have called me for help. "I know. Me, too."

"I IM'd that Asian girl you hang around with to ask for tutoring, but she blew me off. Anyway, that isn't why I called."

Stranger and stranger. "Oh?"

"Me and DeLayne and Emily Overton are throwing a party at Callum's tomorrow night. If you don't have anything else going, maybe you'd like to come."

"I—wow, I—um . . ." I gave myself a mental smack to stop the babbling. "Thanks."

She gave me the address and I wrote it on the back of my class schedule. "So, do you think you'll make it?"

"Maybe," I said cautiously. "Around nine or so."

"Oh, it won't get going until then, at least. And, you know, Brett's going to be there."

I sucked in a breath as if I'd been punched in the stomach. *Please, please, please don't let my hopeless crush be common knowledge.*

Then, in the next second, I knew. Oh, this was just too cruel. Mac had told someone. I'd been so careful not to break her confidence, against my better judgment. But had she done the same?

Obviously not.

I sat on the noisy bus, surrounded by strangers, and felt the hot blood of total mortification seep into my face.

"Hey, Carly, no big deal if you guys are still underground," Christine said. "I'm discreet."

"That's good," I said faintly. What was she talking about?

"I know how totally annoying it is to have people talking about you. Vanessa won't hear about it from me, I promise."

"Okay." People were talking? Did everyone in the whole school know? Had they just invited me so they'd have a captive victim to laugh at? Free entertainment?

"Though I have to warn you, a party at Callum's doesn't happen without her. If you guys show up together—or even separately—be prepared."

"For what?" I rasped from a dry throat.

Christine laughed. "You are so secure. Well, if it were me and I'd just snagged her ex-boyfriend, I'd be arriving in designer Kevlar."

Snagged . . . ?

Boyfriend . . . ?

"Thanks for the heads-up," I said from the depths of the Twilight Zone. There was nothing to do but play along until I found out from someone exactly what was going on.

"No problem. See you there."

" 'Bye."

She rang off, and I realized with a start that I'd missed my stop. I jumped off at the next one and spent the whole five-block walk back trying to figure it out. By the time I got to the school gates, the late spring twilight had deepened into dark, and I was no more enlightened than I'd been before.

I didn't even know who to ask. Certainly not Mac, who had already proved she had a big mouth. And not Lissa or Gillian, who kept a DMZ between themselves and Vanessa's crowd.

Maybe Shani would know. She'd never lie to me, and she wouldn't shrug me off, either. She was pretty hooked into school gossip, mostly because it entertained her. She saw it as her very own walking, talking issue of *Teen People*.

I pushed open the front doors and glanced into the common room as I went by. No Brett. Just as well. I didn't think I could face him if some oh-so-kind person had passed on the latest. Out of habit, I paused in front of the portrait of Eleanor Spencer and gazed at her dress until I felt calmer.

Then I focused.

The Worth gown. Complete with his trademark draping, a waterfall of clever pleats and tucks from shoulder to waist. I leaned closer, trying to see clues in the Impressionist daubs of paint. What if I didn't design a ballgown? What if, with two yards of fabric, I made a cocktail minidress using a design element like this pleating right here? It would be a tip of the hat to Spencer's past, and yet be modern enough to make an entrance at—at TouTou's, for instance.

Carly Aragon, you are a genius.

Brett Loyola and all of his and Vanessa's friends might be laughing at me now, but when I stepped onto the runway in that dress, he'd see me. Really see me. The way he'd seen me the other night, under the trees, when we'd talked about religion. And that wouldn't be all. There'd be designers in that audience with master's degrees in history. They would know where that design element came from. They'd know what I was trying to say.

We'd speak a common language.

Now I just had to make sure the words were perfect.

✣

✉

To: DList_DYD_Committee
From: VTalbot@spenceracad.edu
Date: May 1, 2009
Re: Meeting 2nd period

Hi all. Let's meet at Starbucks today during Life Sciences. I have the final list of designers to share with you, and we've decided on an event planning company. Plans are full speed ahead, so I need to catch you all up.

Vanessa

✉

To: caragon@spenceracad.edu
From: alanaah@mac.com
Date: May 1, 2009
Re: Our dear mama

Hey *hermana menor, que pasa?*

So on the theory that organic waste rolls downhill, Mom is nagging me relentlessly to talk to you about this bridesmaid thing. I don't have a problem standing up with her, but she says you do. Not to play monkey in the middle, but do you want to tell me what's wrong?

I know you don't like Richard, and yeah, Mom walking out on us and getting married again so soon sucks. It's like all these weepy country songs I've been forced to listen to at the studio lately. (Which—OT warning—make me appreciate alt-bluegrass and Tex-Mex even more.) But anyway, the deal is, it's her life. We're making our own way and she's making hers, and let's make the best of it.

My take. Call me if you want.

Love ya,
Alana

. . . .

chapter 12

GIRLFRIEND, WE HAVE to talk."

"Ow!" Shani's bony fingers gripped my elbow so hard that I had trouble shaking her off. "What? I have core class in fifteen minutes."

She hustled me into the common room, which for once was empty. It was Friday morning and everyone was probably still at breakfast.

"It won't take that long for you to give me the scoop. How could you keep this a secret? I thought we were friends."

"Keep what a secret?" The only secrets I had were my job and Mac's mystery e-mail stalker, and it wasn't likely she would have told Shani about that.

What did I know? Mac had blabbed about Brett, so maybe she'd decided to make Drifter this morning's headline, too. If I'd seen her last night, I'd have ripped a strip off her, but I hadn't. I couldn't even tell if she'd come back to our room to sleep because she was gone by the time I woke up that morning.

"Don't play innocent." Shani's brown eyes practically snapped, but with anger or excitement, I couldn't tell. "I got an IM from Gillian yesterday. Apparently you're the big news around here."

I felt my face go cold.

"Oh, come on, don't look so shocked," Shani said. "You're never around, and when you are, you hardly talk. Now with what Gillian says, it all adds up." She crossed her arms over her chest and stuck out a hip. "When were you going to tell me you and Brett had hooked up?"

Out of the corner of my eye, I saw movement at the door. I turned just in time to see blond hair swing out of sight. "Lissa? Is that you?"

Sheepishly, she came back into view. "I wasn't eavesdropping, honest. I was just walking by and thought I heard your voices."

"Don't leave." I motioned her in. "Maybe you can make some sense of what this girl is saying, because I can't."

Shani blew me a raspberry and rolled her eyes. "Don't play coy with me. We haven't seen you in a couple weeks. It's all over school that you and Brett are an item. Since this is, like, your dream come true, I thought you would have at least shared the happy news with us."

I looked from one to the other. "But there isn't any news. No item. I'm not going out with him. I'm not even sure he remembers who I am half the time."

"That's not what I hear." Lissa pulled us farther into the room, close to the hearth. A gas fire usually burned there in the winter, but now that it was May, a big vase of fresh peonies and lilies stood on the tile in front of it. "You've been keeping it pretty clandestine, but now the news is out. I hear you guys let yourselves be seen together the other night, and you're going with him to the party at Callum's."

"I was invited. Like I'd ever go. All I need is for the entire school to know I'm crushing on him."

"The entire school thinks he's crushing on *you*," Shani pointed out.

"Yeah, but the big reveal is that it's all gossip. Why would I want to go to that party and deliberately watch him forget my name in front of everyone? Or worse, not see me at all?"

"You're not going out," Lissa repeated in an I'm-just-clarifying-this tone.

"Are you kidding? He spoke to me on the lawn a couple nights ago. That's it. That's all that happened." She and Shani exchanged a glance. "What? What was that look?"

"Rumor has it that Vanessa found out and her little needle is buried in the red zone," Shani said at last.

"Why should she care?" I demanded. "She kicked him to the curb before spring break."

"I'll tell you what I think." Lissa sat on the upholstered arm of the couch. "I know for a fact she really wants Callum. I bet she's hanging on to Brett to save her pride because Callum can't see her as anything but his buddy from when they were kids."

"Well, someone better tell Brett that," I said, "because as far as I know, he's got a thing for Mac."

"But does she have a thing for him?" Lissa wanted to know.

"I think so," I said. "She's the one who's been out with him and his friends. In fact, I don't think she even came in last night."

Shani's eyes widened. "Now *that's* a headline. Where was she?"

I shrugged. "If they weren't together, then I have no idea. Listen, now that we have this cleared up, I have to get to core class."

"Watch your back," Shani warned. "We may know the truth, and you may know the truth, but Vanessa and the rest of the school don't know it."

I nodded and gave them both the warmest smile I could muster, then headed down the corridor. On top of everything else, now this? At least my feelings for Brett weren't public knowledge. If they were gossiping about us going out, that implied people thought he had feelings for me. I knew he didn't, but at least my pride wouldn't go down in a gale of laughter.

Concentrating on History of the Ancient World was nearly impossible, so it was a relief to get out and head for Life Sciences and my fashion-design elective. I could think of no better way to lose all my stress than to immerse myself in plans for my dress. As I approached the door, I was so busy compiling a list in my head of the materials I'd need for the hands-on part of the class, which happened after the lecture, that I didn't see Emily Overton until I practically walked into her.

"Hey," she said. "Just the person I was looking for. Are you coming?"

"Hi. Coming where?"

"To the DYD meeting. Vanessa sent an e-mail last night. Didn't you get it?"

I shook my head. "I haven't checked my mail since yesterday afternoon."

"It's a good thing I ran into you, then. Come on. It's at Starbucks."

I glanced frantically into the classroom, with its pattern-drafting equipment and dress forms and yards of muslin for experimenting, all waiting for me. "I—I—wait, Emily." I shook my arm free of her leechy grip.

"What's to wait for?" she demanded. "The Life Sciences teachers all know what we're doing. It's not like you're going to get a demerit."

Two girls pushed past us, and commandeered a dress form. That left four. If I didn't lose Emily, they'd all be gone. "It's not that. It's just that I, um . . . I really need to do some work in here today."

"And Vanessa really needs us to know what's going on. Don't you want to hear who the designers are going to be?"

Sure, but that would be common knowledge by dinnertime. And the meeting? They'd order their extra-hot nonfat no-whip lattes and spend forty-five seconds on an update and the rest of the time talking about me and Brett—right in front of us. And truthfully, I could go a few more days without seeing Vanessa. At least until her needle got back down into the black, you know what I mean?

I stepped past Emily and into the classroom. "Tell her I'm sorry, okay?"

"Okay," Emily said slowly. "But she's not going to be happy that you blew her off."

"You said that sometimes the boys don't come. What's the difference?"

"They're boys. All the girls come."

"Well, I can't," I said firmly. I was taking a calculated risk, but I needed to get my hands on some muslin, stat. Besides, even if Vanessa did want to cut me from the committee, she'd have Mac to deal with. We were showing definite signs of becoming friends, what with all the secrets between us, and she'd want me to stay. "I'll see you later."

And I headed over to the window to bag a dress form before she could say another word. As I sat through a pretty interesting lecture on how to turn a tailored collar and afterward began the hands-on work with the form and my muslin, pleating and draping and marking cutting lines, keeping Eleanor Spencer's dress in my mind's eye for reference, a sense of calm began to wash away the edge of my anxiety.

Gillian once told me she talked to God all the time, in her head. Asking Him to walk her through tense moments. Thanking Him for good things. I remember thinking at the time that she had some nerve, yakking away to the Creator of everything like they were best buds.

But maybe there was something in it.

You are here with me, Father. Thank You for helping me see that. Thank You for this class and for letting me discover something that I really love to do.

Help me figure out how to handle this Brett rumor. If I have to look like an idiot because of my feelings, help me get through it gracefully.

And help me know what to do about Drifter. I don't like the sound of him, Father. I'm asking for Your protection here and Your hand around Mac. I don't think she believes in You, but for my sake, could You keep an eye on her? Thanks, Lord.

Gillian was right. Prayer wasn't something you had to do. It was something you loved to do. I felt twenty times better after putting my problems in front of God. I might be clumsy and undecided and not very well equipped to handle things, but He wasn't. He had everything I needed—I just had to ask.

During dance practice, I felt so confident that I got through a complicated hip-hop routine with only one mistake. "Nice work, Miss Aragon," the instructor called to me. "A few more performances like that and you'll be ready for the recital in June— which, may I remind you all, is your final exam."

At lunch, I grabbed a panini sandwich and stopped by Lissa's and Shani's table. "I have so much homework I'm just going to go out in the quad and work all afternoon," I told them. "If I don't see you, have a good weekend."

"Are you going down to San Jose?" Shani asked. "And blowing off that party?"

I slid right past the first question, since I'd be going to work as usual at four, and answered the second. "I wouldn't go on a bet. If they want entertainment, they can hire a juggler or a trained monkey. I have better things to do."

"Good for you." Lissa air-clapped for me. "Nine out of ten people here would sell their little brothers for an invitation."

I had to laugh. "Antony may be a pain, but he's worth more than that. Hey, has anyone seen Mac yet?"

"She stumbled into core class looking like the morning after," Lissa said. "No books. She had to borrow a piece of paper from me to take notes on. Maybe your grades don't count in an exchange term."

"Oh, I think they do," Shani said. "I'll bet she gets an A in Party 101."

"What did your teacher say?" I asked.

Lissa shrugged. "He handed her his textbook and asked her to stand up and read a sonnet. Which she did, flawlessly. I think he just likes to listen to her accent."

It must be nice to party all night and use charm and your friends' notes to pass your classes. *Mac and her classes aren't your problem. Neither is her stalker. She won't let them be your problem, so just let it go.*

"See you guys later."

I found an empty table in a sunny part of the quad and did a fast triage on my homework assignments. Just how much could I get done before I caught the three-thirty bus to work? AP Chem: that could wait for study group Sunday night. English: Read a chapter of the textbook and the first ten chapters of *Clarissa*. I could do that tomorrow before I went to sleep. Spanish: vocab, no problem. A quick review before class and I'd be good to go. Math: the end-of-chapter test.

Groan. I could feel the headache coming on already.

But it wasn't like I could put it off. Mr. Jackson, our math teacher, was relentless, and she who fell behind got left behind. Resigning myself to the pain, I got to work.

An hour later a shadow fell across my books and I looked up.

"Trying for the Dean's list?" Brett Loyola asked.

I stared into that smile, which was at least as dazzling as the sun behind his head, and lost the ability to speak. He sat down opposite me as though a star-struck female wasn't anything unusual—which it probably wasn't—and turned my textbook toward him to see what I was working on.

"Math," he said in a knowing tone. "But you've done the word problems, right?"

I nodded. "Another week and we're moving on to trig. If we all survive that long."

He laughed. "Most girls wouldn't be happy about that."

"I like something I can visualize on paper. Give me a triangle or the volume of water in a pipe and I'm good. Word problems just confuse me."

"I had to give Christine Powell emergency tutoring to get her through her first midterm. She's in worse shape than you."

I bet.

"So, what are you up to?" I amazed myself, sounding so casual. As if the very sight of him sitting in front of me, his arms crossed on the table, didn't make me forget to breathe. Heroically, I resisted the urge to dabble my fingers in his shadow, which fell across my papers just inches from my pencil.

"I just got done with crew and saw you out here, working away."

Do not blush. Do not. "I have a busy weekend, so I wanted to get as much done now as I could. You know how Jackson is. He told us fifty times he does the Bay to Breakers marathon. He thinks math is something you train for, too. 'You have to do it every day.'" I mimicked Mr. Jackson's beefy voice.

To my amazement, Brett laughed. "Busy weekend, huh? Whatcha got going?"

Stories—okay, fibs—flapped in my skull like a flock of birds. I shook them off. "Just stuff. Personal stuff."

"I see," he said knowingly, as if that were code for something else. Like a mad, passionate affair, maybe. Uh-huh. That was *so* me. "So are you coming to the party?"

I swallowed. "I hadn't really thought about it." Not after I'd decided not to go.

"Christine invited you, right?"

"Well, yes, but—"

"I get it. More personal stuff?"

Had he heard the rumors or not? And if he had, how did he feel? What did he think of me? Did he think of me at all?

"Look, Brett, this is kind of awkward." I sounded desperately uncomfortable. I knew that. But I plunged on anyway, knowing it would shoot down any chance at all of him seeing me the way I wanted him to. "There's a rumor going around. About—about you. And me. About us."

Oh, Lord. I need You now. Please help me to not be such a dork.

"Yeah?"

He hadn't heard. I felt like banging my head on the table. Why hadn't I kept my mouth shut?

"Maybe you haven't heard it. Anyway. I—I wanted you to know I didn't start it. I don't know who did. Someone with a big imagination and nothing to do, I guess."

"Someone is always spreading rumors. You get used to it. Don't let it bother you, Carly."

My name. Ohmigosh, he remembered my name!

"It does bother me. Did. Because it involved you. And it wasn't true."

Could I sound any more idiotic? He was going to wonder how I got past the admissions board, at this rate.

"Are you so sure about that?"

I stared at him. "About what?"

"That it isn't true. Because I was hoping you'd go with me."

Welcome back to the Twilight Zone, ladies and gentlemen. I'm your host, Carly Aragon, and I've just been abducted by aliens and replaced by a popular fashionista on whom Brett Loyola would appear to have a crush.

CAragon   Hola, Enrique. Cancel tonight's pickup, OK?

LimoGuy   That's 3 in a row. Esta OK?

CAragon   Totally OK. Hot date.

LimoGuy   You tell him he'd better be good to you or he answers to me.

CAragon   I love you too, Enrique.

chapter 13

HI, PAPA, it's me."

My father took me off his office speakerphone right away and picked up the receiver. "Carolina, it's good to hear your voice. I'm looking forward to seeing you tonight."

I moistened my lips and chose my words carefully. "Actually, that's why I'm calling. Would it be okay if I came home Saturday night instead?"

"Saturday? But that would only give us Sunday together, and then Enrique comes at five. What's going on that's more important than being with Antony and me?"

"Um . . . I have a date."

Silence fell while my father digested the unthinkable. "A date? With a boy? Do I know him?"

"Of course with a boy, and no, you haven't met him personally, but you've seen him. At the Benefactors' Day Ball in October."

"I don't remember."

"He was dancing with the committee chair. Tall, dark hair, very handsome. His name is Brett Loyola and his family owns a bunch of restaurants and things up here."

"Loyola? Wasn't there a mayor by that name?"

"That was his *abuelito*."

"I see."

"He's really nice, Papa."

"If he's so nice, why haven't I met him? You know how important it is to me that I know who your friends are."

I bit down on the urge to say, *Because you're never here*. "He only asked me this afternoon." And I was still expecting to get a text message that said:

TEXT MESSAGE ━━━━━━━━━━━━━━━━━━━━━━━━━━━━━━━━━━━━━━━

Brett Loyola   Kidding! How about those chem notes?

━━━

"And what's the event?"

"We're going to a"—*don't say party, he'll freak*—"walking over to his friend Callum's house. My roommate is going, too, and the girls who are on the Design Your Dreams committee with me."

"Will there be adults there?"

"Callum's mom and grandmother." I hoped. I didn't actually know. "Papa, it's not like I'm thirteen and we'll be playing Spin the Bottle. It's just an evening at Callum's house to listen to music and talk."

"If they start drinking, you're to go back to school right away."

I rolled my eyes. "Yes, Papa."

"That kind of thing is all too likely. I want you to take a picture of the mother and grandmother with your phone and send it to me, so I know there are adults there."

"Papa!"

"Don't use that tone of voice with me, young lady. If that offends you, then I want you to have one of them call me."

"You might as well put my hair in pigtails and give me a lollipop."

"What is that supposed to mean?"

I took a long breath and tried to sound mature and reasonable. "I'm not a baby, Papa. I'm nearly seventeen and it's just a group of friends getting together. If I go around taking pictures of people's parents, I'll never live it down."

"Then you're not going."

There's only so much a girl can take. I'd been dealing with a lot of stress, with classes, with Mac and Drifter and Brett. But even leaving all that out, I'd been practically on my own for nine months. I was running my life just fine without parental supervision, thank you very much. I was trustworthy, practical, and responsible—everything he wanted me to be. And this was how he treated me? "No? You're sixty miles away."

"Carolina Isabella!"

I choked. I'd gone too far. "I'm sorry, Papa. I didn't mean that."

"I should hope not. If this disrespect and rebellion are the result of going to that fancy school, I'm pulling you out of there."

"Please don't. I like it here. I earned it."

"Then I want you to remember where you came from. Your mother and I brought you up better than this."

"I know, Papa."

"So, I'll see you Saturday morning, then. I'll tell Enrique to pick you up at, what, ten o'clock? Will you be recovered from your party by then?"

Uh-oh. "Don't bother Enrique. I'll just catch the train. I'll let you know which one, and you can pick me up in Fremont." That was just half an hour from the condo.

"What's the matter with Enrique?"

"Nothing, except the poor guy might want a life. He doesn't

have to give up a Saturday to cart me around when I can take the train practically from the doorstep."

My father mulled this over, and I tried not to tap my fingers on my desk, in case he could hear me. "Fine," he said at last. "You can take the train this once, and I'll meet you at the Fremont station at noon."

"Um . . ."

"Now what?" My father had already come within inches of losing it, and I couldn't afford to have him go over the edge. At the same time, I couldn't afford to skip a full Saturday of work, either.

"It might be a little later than noon."

"Do you plan to sleep the entire day away? Is that more important than seeing your family?"

"Of course not. I just have some things to do."

"What kind of things?"

Calm. Reasonable. Responsible. "Papa, I'll be done at four. I'll take the train and be there in time to make supper."

"What will you be done with at four? What are you hiding from me?"

"I'm not hiding anything! I have a job, that's all, and I work until four on Saturdays."

"You . . . *what*?"

I ran my free hand through my bangs in exasperation. You'd think I'd just confessed to a drive-by shooting. *Calm. Reasonable.* "I work in a photography store in the afternoons, and all day Saturday. So I may as well tell you, this will be a regular thing."

"Reg—work—you work? In a store? Carolina, what are you thinking?"

"You don't have to shout. It's nothing to be ashamed of."

"You are in school. You are to be focused on that. What in heaven's name do you need to work for?"

"I need the money."

"I will give you money!"

"You can't give me enough to buy fabric from London and a pair of Jimmy Choo shoes, Papa. That's what I need to walk down the runway at the Design Your Dreams show."

"No one *needs* such garbage."

"Maybe not in your world, but in my world, they do. So I got a job to pay for it. I'm being a responsible adult. And I like it."

"I don't care whether you like it or not. You call your boss immediately and tell him you quit. I will meet your train tomorrow at noon and we will discuss this."

I would *not* be told what to do when this was so important. "What you mean is, *you* will discuss it. You taught us to be independent and to work for the things we want. Well, I'm doing just what you taught me. I'm old enough to make my own decisions, and there's nothing wrong with what I've decided."

"Carolina, you listen to—"

But I never heard what I was to listen to. I snapped my phone shut and turned it off, and unplugged the room extension, too, for good measure.

My father had nothing to complain about. I didn't do drugs; I didn't drink; I didn't do anything but win scholarships and get good grades and make him proud. All I wanted was this one little thing, and he treated it like I was making extra cash by selling crack on the street corner.

Well, I was going to keep my job, and I was going to go to that party, and he could just get used to it. Maybe I'd be on that evening train to Fremont and maybe I wouldn't. Either way, I made the decisions, not him. I was old enough to take control of my life, and that was that.

Something moved behind me, and I whirled around in my chair. Mac stood there, leaning on the door.

I gasped, half in surprise, half in sudden fear of what she might have heard. "When did you come in? How long have you been there?"

"Long enough," she drawled. "Having growing pains? Carly

Aragon's secret life. Who knew that her deep, dark secret was . . . a job in a photo shop?"

"That's none of your business!" I snapped. Then I looked at her more closely. "Weren't you wearing that yesterday?"

"Give the girl a gold star." She stripped off a denim mini that didn't even come close to meeting the finger test, and unbuttoned her school blouse, which looked as if she'd slept in it.

"Mac, are you okay?"

"Oh, I'm just peachy."

"You didn't sleep here last night."

She snorted. "Just figuring that out, are you?"

My own needle dropped abruptly back into the red zone. "Look, I just got off the phone with my father. I don't need you giving me attitude, too. I'm trying to be your friend, you idiot, not preach at you. Now, are you okay or not?"

Half into her skinny jeans, she stared at me. And before my eyes, all the snot and vinegar went out of her, and her face wavered. She looked about twelve years old, afraid and vulnerable. "No, I'm not," she said in a high, unsteady voice, and two big tears rolled down her cheeks as she pulled her jeans on the rest of the way and yanked on a T-shirt.

All my own attitude vanished like fog under the sun. "Oh, girlfriend, come here." I put my arms around her and sat beside her on the bed. "Tell me what's wrong."

In answer, she retrieved her laptop from her bag and flipped it open. "Read that."

....

✉

To: lmacphail@spenceracad.edu
From: drifter1989@gmail.com
Date: May 1, 2009
Re: Kiss the girls

It's such a shame that *Hello!* and the *Sun* don't do you justice. I could—and have—done a better job of shooting you. Ha! I mean, photographing you. Those aristocratic genes can overcome even a school uniform. Wish I'd gotten some of them.

I'm looking forward to the day we meet. I've known about you for a couple of years, but if I hadn't reached out, you'd never have heard of me. Might want to ask His Lordship what he was up to twenty years ago. That'll give you a clue about a lot of things. Including the Big Divorce.

In the meantime, enjoy your classes and your friends. Boyfriend, too, huh? You didn't waste any time. But maybe that's a good thing. I'm very unhappy that you don't talk to me. I'm the one person in the world you need to talk to. Maybe I'm not important to you. Yet. Your days are numbered, you see.

Every

  last

    one.

Drifter

....

I couldn't draw enough breath into my lungs. "I'm going to say this one more time. You *have* to tell someone."

Mac didn't meet my eyes. "Want to know where I spent the night?"

If she said "At Brett's," I didn't know what I'd do. "Where?"

"At the St. Francis Hotel. I was so frightened that I called a cab and told him to take me anywhere—just as long as it was far away from here. I walked and walked through crowds of tourists and finally wound up there. No luggage." She made a sound that might have been a laugh. "They thought I looked a bit dodgy, but my Platinum Visa convinced them otherwise."

I could buy those shoes I needed for the price of a night at the St. Francis. "But, Mac, why? Why don't you just tell Ms. Curzon and let campus security take care of it?"

"What could they do? I don't have any idea who Drifter is or what he looks like. And all you remember is that he had on a hoodie. What am I supposed to tell them?"

"That he's threatening you. 'Your days are numbered.' At least they could have someone assigned to protect you."

"What, like a bodyguard? I'm not royalty. And nobody's going to take a nutter like this seriously. I'm sure lots of people at this school get the same annoyances."

"He's not an annoyance. He's watching you. He knows what you're *wearing*, Mac. He's close enough to take pictures. That's just scary. You have to be sensible and tell someone. If you don't, I will."

She gripped my wrist, hard. "Don't do that, Carly."

"Please don't tell me you don't want the papers to find out."

She shook her head. "I don't care about the rags. It's my dad."

"You don't want your dad to find out?" If he were like mine, he'd be on the next plane over, ready to hunt Drifter down.

"No. Didn't you see what he said? My dad did something wrong twenty years ago. Who knows what—some business deal, some lawsuit, I don't know. If I go to the police or tell anyone, it will rake all that up. He's been through the most awful time, Carly. With the divorce and maybe losing Strathcairn and every-thing. I just don't have the heart to make it worse for him."

"But . . ." My voice trailed away.

"Thank you for being such a good friend." Now it was Mac hugging me. "But we just have to hope that if I ignore him, Drifter will go away."

"I'd say he was doing the opposite of that."

"I just need to keep my head down and make sure I don't go anywhere alone. Right?"

"I suppose, but—"

"So. About this party tonight. Do you mind if I tag along?"

The girl had just gotten a death threat. What could I say? "Of course not. You can come with Brett and me."

ON THE FIRST two floors, Callum McCloud's house looked like something out of a movie. You know how some people seem to hit their high point, say, in high school, and the rest of their life is just a rehash of the good old days? His house was like that. It seemed to me it had hit its high point in the twenties or thirties, and everything after that was second rate.

But on the third floor . . . that was Callum's space, and you could tell it had been remodeled with parties in mind. Bright and open, with maple floors made for dancing, it had the biggest flat-screen plasma TV I'd ever seen mounted on one wall. Squashy couches were scattered in front of it, and a low, square glass table held munchies in glass bowls. If you wanted to play games on the Wii, you could do that on a second TV on the other end, where the exercise machines were. His music system took up another wall, and kids took turns plugging the party mixes on their iPods into it and voting on who had the best one.

For a guy who kept a low profile, Callum was surprisingly well set up to entertain. To my relief, I did get a brief glimpse of a woman I assumed was his mother, tucked away in a study watching the news, but she neither spoke to us nor looked up when a Hispanic woman led us to the stairs.

"*Gracias, señora,*" I said as Brett, Mac, and I started up. The woman looked surprised. Maybe she wasn't used to being thanked. Or maybe I'd made a bad assumption and she didn't speak Spanish.

Would you think I was totally lame if I admitted this was the first real party I'd ever been to? I mean, the first that wasn't mostly family?

Although it did have something in common with a family party—if I'd walked into our old house with Brett Loyola, a silence like this would have fallen with a crash as people stared and the music thumped. But in this case, no parents, aunts, and uncles came rushing over to meet my date and give him the third degree about his family, his education, his prospects, and his intentions.

In about three seconds, people resumed their conversations and watched out of the corners of their eyes as Brett crossed the room to get us drinks. I took courage from the flawlessly cut Thakoon silk dress I'd begged from Gillian at the last minute. I had to live up to it—to wear it like an old T-shirt I'd known and loved for a long time. Mac had done my makeup, so I knew I looked good. No one would guess that Brett's date was a scholarship student who worked in a photo shop, would they?

"Thanks." I smiled up at him as I took the soda he offered me. There was probably alcohol circulating around the room, but I didn't want to know about it. All I wanted was for more people to get up and dance so Brett would ask me, too.

"Want some munchies?" Brett asked. "Carmela makes the best salsa and dips you ever had."

"Who's Carmela?"

"The woman who answered the door. Their housekeeper."

"Oh. No, thanks." I was too keyed up to eat, and besides, I'd split a submarine sandwich with Phillip earlier, during our supper break.

"My man." Callum McCloud clapped Brett on the back and grinned at Mac and me. "Trust you to arrive with the two hottest ladies in school."

I knew he was just saying that, but at the same time, I felt a blush rising in my face. Mac just gave him a lazy look. She probably heard that kind of thing all the time.

Off to my left, I heard someone go "Shhh!" and then a husky voice said, "Brett! What a surprise."

I turned to see Vanessa Talbot, looking amazing in the exact same Narcisco Rodriguez dress that Natalie Portman had worn to the premiere of her new movie the week before. Only Vanessa's was made in dark purple chiffon instead of green silk.

"Hey, Vanessa," he greeted her, a little coldly, I thought. "No surprise."

"Oh, not to see you," she said. "Just who else you let in." From her expression, we were a couple of trolls he'd picked up in the Tenderloin on the way over. "Were you invited?" she asked me.

"A couple of times." Wow, was that really me? I sounded as cool and bored as Mac. "But I only decided to come when Brett asked me."

Someone behind me sucked in a breath.

"Really." Vanessa looked me up and down, but thanks to Mac and Gillian's work, she couldn't find anything to criticize. She lifted her gaze to his. "I didn't know you specialized in minority cases."

"Oooooh," someone in the back said, just under the level of the music.

"Get over it, Van," Brett said. "Carly and Mac are doing me a favor. Otherwise I might be stuck with, you know, whoever turned up." *Like you just did*, his tone said.

"You're stuck, I'll give you that." A little on the lame side, and she knew it, because she turned her back on the three of us and flounced away.

"Exes," Brett muttered, but he didn't say any more, because at that moment Los Lonely Boys began to sing. The salsa beat infected a bunch of people, who flooded into the space that had been cleared. Seconds later, I realized I was beating out the pattern with my high heels, the hem of my minidress brushing my thighs just the way it was designed to do.

This was my kind of stuff. The music I'd grown up with—the rhythms that had filled our house and that had moved me to dance when I'd been barely old enough to walk.

"Want to dance?" Brett asked, and I turned, my lips parting to say yes, my feet moving, my hips already swinging to the beat.

"Sure," Mac said, smiling up into his eyes.

I watched, my mouth still open on that yes, as my date led my roommate out onto the floor and she shimmied into his arms.

chapter 14

"HOW ABOUT IT?"

I dragged my gaze off the two of them and found Callum McCloud at my shoulder. "What?"

"Dance with me?" It was a good thing he didn't wait for an answer, because I wasn't capable of one. Instead, he grabbed my hand as though he expected a yes, and the music and my body took over. And you know what?

We were totally hot.

Callum McCloud, say what you will about his lack of a moral center, is a terrific dancer—and the salsa is my favorite. Between the two of us, we burned up that floor, and soon people were standing out of the way to give us room. She may have a wardrobe to die for and a Platinum Visa, but when it comes to Latin dancing and hip-hop, well, Mac probably does a really good Sir Roger de Coverley, you know?

Because even Brett was staring at me over her shoulder like he'd never seen me before.

My hair whipped back and forth, my heels drummed with cocky abandon, and my hips moved on greased ball bearings.

Even at three hundred pounds, my Tía Margarita can dance the shoes off any man, and she taught all her nieces well. The salsa segued into *la bamba* and then into reggaeton, where I could throw in a few cha-cha hip rolls and even hint at a *paso doble*, then broke to crunk and old-school, and I danced them all.

And not with Callum, either. He got the first two, and then was elbowed out of the way by some guy whose name I didn't even catch. Someone—Christine Powell, I think—plugged in a house mix and still the partners kept coming. It wasn't until the music slowed to Rihanna singing a soulful ballad that Brett finally pulled Todd Runyon away from me and directed him into the crowd with a firm push to the back.

"Finally," he said. And finally I walked into his arms.

The funny thing was, it didn't feel the way I'd expected it to. Our feet were just a touch out of sync, and instead of moving like one person, our knees knocked together. "Sorry," he murmured.

Under my cheek, his linen jacket smelled fresh and his cologne was nice, but . . . *Oh, come on Carly. Your dream has just come true. What more can you possibly want?*

I don't know . . . maybe if I hadn't been the consolation prize—if he'd chosen me first—the romantic glow wouldn't have faded to the ridiculous reality of knocking knees and crunched toes.

You're never satisfied. Nothing's ever good enough. Not your parents' living arrangements, your wardrobe, your roommate. What's the matter with you?

Being the one he'd danced with first would have been good enough.

That wasn't too much to ask, was it?

I WATCHED THE PHOTOGRAPHS drop out of the developing machine and into the catch slot with metronome regularity.

Pish. Pish. Pish. Like a clock designed to put you to sleep instead of wake you up.

You know how you get a song in your head and you can't get rid of it? Earworms, they call them. Well, I was having mindworms. No matter what I did, changing views of Mac dancing in Brett's arms superimposed themselves over what I was doing, like one movie playing on top of another.

The boredom of processing photographs did not help the situation.

Pish. Pish.

I'd left the party around eleven-thirty and walked back to school with a guy and two girls I didn't know from the senior class. I'd cracked open an eye when Mac tiptoed in and my digital clock had said 3:14. Consequently, she was still rolled up under the covers when I left for work.

Had Brett walked her back to school or called her a cab? I didn't know, and you know what? It didn't matter anymore.

I'd still admire him from a distance, because face it, the guy is just yummy—but any hope of being the girl he chose first, of seeing that smile reserved just for me, had evaporated when he'd asked Mac to dance. He'd chosen her instead of me in front of all his friends, so hey, I can pull a clue out of the clue jar and read it.

Pish.

The last of the customer's pictures settled into the tray and I gathered them up, glancing through them as I fanned them into order in my hands.

Then I blinked. I gazed at the top photo for several seconds while my mind processed what I was seeing.

A close-up of a pipe.

Packing material. A fuse, shot in macro detail.

No biggie. The guy was probably a plumber. People take pictures of the stuff they use for work. They take pictures of food.

Of their bathroom cabinets. Vacations, school trips, kids, pets. Shoes. Those are big. Shoes on other people who don't know they're being photographed. Body parts, too—especially body parts of people who don't know anyone is looking. Very popular, those.

Yeah, after nearly a month processing images of the things people thought were important enough to record and keep, I was pretty much jaded to the weirdness factor.

I flipped through a couple more pictures. Firecrackers. Big ones. Tied together with wire. Uh, not a close-up, if the discarded sneakers next to the stack were life-size. I peered at the photo, held it up to the light.

Those were sticks of dynamite. Even I could tell that, and the closest I've ever gotten to one was on Gillian's *CSI* DVDs.

Okay, not a plumber. Construction guy? Demolition specialist? Cop? Were these pictures of some kind of raid? No, police departments had their own developing equipment, didn't they? They didn't need to use Piccadilly Photo.

I glanced at the clock. A quarter to noon, and the checkbox on the customer's envelope said he'd pick them up at noon or later. Philip was a total hardnose about having the pictures processed on time or before, so I had to hurry.

But the weirdness factor here was higher than usual, and a strange, cold anxiety began to coil in my stomach.

A bunch of canisters all taped together, with "LP Gas" lettered on the side.

More pipes, their ends packed neatly, stacked up in neat pyramids like kindling.

Is that what pipe bombs look like?

And guns. Even I could tell a sawed-off shotgun when I saw it. Antony has watched a zillion Bruce Willis and Arnold Schwarzenegger movies where people shot off guns that looked just like this. The last several pictures showed a guy with brown hair standing in front of a map, and in the last picture in the stack, he held up a handgun in a kind of salute.

I frowned at the picture. The guy was a complete stranger. Wasn't he?

I glanced at the clock. Five to twelve. I don't think I even made a conscious decision. I just programmed the developing machine to print another set of pictures.

The bell over the door jingled when there were half a dozen yet to go.

"Can I help you?" I heard Philip ask.

"Yeah, I'm here to pick up my photographs," said a male voice. He sounded young, and his accent was odd. Not British, like the ones in all my historical DVDs, and not Scottish like Mac. I couldn't place it. And he said the words slowly, as though he thought Philip couldn't hear. "The name's Strathey."

I stifled a sound. The name on the envelope I'd just processed. Twice.

"Certainly." Envelopes slapped each other gently as Philip flipped through the drawer that held orders for pickup. I grabbed the first set of pictures and stuffed them into their envelope, and stashed them at the very bottom of my tote. Then I opened another envelope, scribbled "Strathey" and an illegible phone number at the top, and was standing calmly by the finishing tray as Philip stepped through the door.

"Carly, are those the Strathey order?"

Pish.

The last of the photos dropped into the tray and I picked them up. "Yes. Just let me get the negatives."

"Cutting it a little close, aren't you?" he asked.

"Sorry," I mumbled, fishing out negatives and stuffing them into their own envelope. "Lots of orders to process today."

"And what have I told you about that?"

"To do them in order of pickup." I handed him the completed order. "I'm sorry, Philip. It won't happen again."

He smiled, looking at me closely. I tried to relax my shoulders and not look as panicked as I felt. "It's all right. I'm not castigating you. Most people don't come on the tick of the dot to pick up their photographs, anyway, do they?"

Not unless you were a crazed gun-happy psychopath bomber.

I followed Philip through the door and watched him hand the envelope to the guy fidgeting in front of the counter, who paid in cash. It was the guy in the pictures, all right. He looked younger in real life. Skinnier. Less threatening.

The sun shone through the shop windows as he left, falling on a gray hoodie that looked way too warm for an almost-summer day, and lighting his hair so that it turned auburn, almost red. He walked up the hill, passing by the window and out of sight.

A gray hoodie. Photographs.

No, it couldn't be the same person. It was just some random plumber guy. People didn't just collect stuff and make bombs in their bedrooms . . . Oh, who was I fooling? Just because I'd never gone to a school that had suffered a shooting or a bombing, didn't mean it couldn't happen in a city where I lived.

"Carly? Are you going to stand there all day, or do we have more orders back there?"

"Yes, Philip."

Like a robot, I turned and went back to work.

Only now, the movie in my head was one hundred percent weird, with explosions and guns and fear—and starred the skinny kid in the gray hoodie.

JUST HOW WEIRD did weirdness have to get before you were morally obligated to do something about it?

I finally understood why Mac felt the way she did about the Drifter problem. No, she wasn't actually being harmed. No one was hurting her. But you could feel both harmed and hurt without the guy laying a finger on you.

That, I realized suddenly, was what had happened to Gillian last term. Lucas Hayes had systematically torn her down on the inside before he got started on her outside by throwing her into a soda machine (among other things).

This was how guys like Drifter and Lucas worked. They messed you up in your mind until you were almost expecting things to get worse. And when they finally did, you were left going, "Yep, I was right," and wondering if somehow you'd brought this on yourself. Or if you deserved it.

Mac wound up feeling hunted, and I felt scared and threatened. Well, neither Mac nor I deserved to feel this way. She'd done nothing to warrant getting those creepy, threatening e-mail messages, and I'd found these pictures by accident. There'd been a fifty-fifty chance that Philip might have developed them, after all.

The question was, what could I do?

Are you brain-dead? Go to the cops, of course.

And say what? That I'd massively invaded someone's privacy by looking through their pictures and making a second copy for myself?

Ouch.

I needed to talk to someone. Philip was the obvious place to start, but for all I knew, he'd fire me for the aforementioned invasion of privacy. I could tell my father, but he wasn't over my having a job yet. He'd probably get so into lecturing me that I'd never get his attention on the actual problem. I needed a neutral party.

I needed my friends.

What I got was Mac.

I pushed open the door of our room, intending to drop off my tote bag and run up to Shani's room. Instead, I found Mac curled up almost the way I'd left her, except dressed and on top of the covers. Her laptop sat on one end of the bed.

She shivered, and in the silence I heard a muffled sob.

"Mac? Are you okay?"

"No-o-o," she wailed into the blanket.

I forgot that she'd spent the whole previous evening in the arms of the guy I wanted. I forgot that I'd invited her along with us to be nice and she'd stabbed me in the back. I forgot that she'd come in at three o'clock after doing who knows what with him.

I put my arms around her. "Mac. *Chica*, what is it? What's happened? Did somebody hurt you? Tell me."

In answer, she sobbed harder, her face flushed red and her cheeks slick with tears. A horrible thought struck me.

"Is everything okay at home? Did something happen to your mom? Or your dad?"

"No." Gasp. "No." Smaller gasp. She sat up and pushed her hair out of her face. Her lips trembled and she could hardly breathe.

I got a handful of tissues and she blew her nose. "Thanks."

"Please tell me. Whatever it is, you can't go through it alone."

That set her off again, and it was a few minutes before she calmed down enough to be coherent. She pulled the laptop over and opened it. "It's him."

I didn't need to ask.

....

✉

To: lmacphail@spenceracad.edu
From: drifter1989@gmail.com

Date: May 2, 2009
Re: Long lost

I hope you enjoyed your party last night. You stayed out pretty late, bad girl. Do that lad and your pretty brunette friend know what kind of family you come from?

Maybe I should explain. I told you once that you don't know me, but I've known about you for a while. I followed you to America to fix this. I could have done it while you were in London, but looking at it now, this is much better. America has such a good rep for this stuff. And as people here would say, Columbine is so yesterday. They need something new to talk about.

Where was I? Oh, yeah. Introducing myself. Have you asked your father what he was up to twenty years ago? Probably not, or I would have heard. Basically, he was a very bad boy, and I'm the result.

Surprised? So was I. Wow—the illegitimate son of the Earl of Strathcairn. No expensive private school for me—just the local comp. No designer clothes, only what we could dig out of the bin at the church jumble sale. No restaurant meals—unless you count the fish and chips at the pub in Newcastle where my mum works. Has worked since our dad dumped her and took up with Her Ladyship.

So instead of me being Viscount Strathey and the heir to Strathcairn, there's you and your meaningless title, since Debrett's says the old pile is entailed to some cousin when Papa kicks off. I don't see the point in either of us.

I want us to do something really amazing together. To go out in a blaze of glory. People will talk about us for years to come. That's way better than what you have to look forward to: a sad little life full of meaningless cocktail parties and relationships that fizzle out like leftover champagne. Isn't it?

Your brother,
David Nelson aka Drifter

. . . .

chapter 15

NEVER IN A MILLION years could I have anticipated *this*.

In the few seconds it had taken me to read the e-mail, Mac had gotten a grip on herself. She blew her nose again, and when she'd tossed the tissue in the trash, she took a deep breath that somehow said, "There. That's over with."

"Of course I called my dad," she said. "Everything he—Drifter—says is, apparently, true."

"I'd kind of hoped he was just delusional," I said softly. "Misguided and weird and OCD."

"Oh, I think he's all that. But he's also quite right. Daddy had an affair with a woman called Lisbet Nelson in 1987, when he was plain Graham MacPhail and fresh out of university. She was married; he was young. At least, that's how he excuses it. I'm not feeling very charitable about boyish mistakes at the moment."

"Was he ever planning to tell you?"

"No," she said grimly. "Even though Drifter's mother apparently clued him in a couple of years ago. I don't know why she bothered. But at least I know now why my parents split up. I just wish they'd thought enough of me to share it."

"They were probably just trying to protect you. This David . . . He seems to think he's entitled to your life. Or at least what you've got," I said thoughtfully, reading the e-mail again.

"He's welcome to it."

"You don't mean that, Mac." I thought of the Balenciagas and the Chanel Couture dress. "Your folks obviously wanted the best for you, and they could afford it. Where's the harm?"

She shot a meaningful glance at the laptop, and I got the message.

"You're not responsible for him being a jealous psycho," I said. "If you're feeling that way, get over it right now."

"What I'm *feeling* is furious at my father," she snapped, moving away from me a little. "This is *his* fault, the irresponsible git."

"It's his fault you have a brother you never knew about," I told her. "But it's not his fault Drifter got all whacked and came to California to do . . . what, exactly?" I read the e-mail again. "This is more than just watching you. I don't like this stuff about Columbine. Not one bit."

Something pinged in my memory, but I couldn't pin it down.

"I'm not very keen about going out in a blaze of glory, either." She sounded more subdued, as if she regretted the snap.

I looked at her. "I'm only going to say this one more time."

"I know. I know. But at least we have more to go on now. Like a name. And this."

She swung the laptop toward herself and opened an attachment I hadn't seen at the bottom of the e-mail. An image filled the screen.

My mouth fell open.

"That's him? That's Drifter? David whatsisname?"

And suddenly everything fell into place, the puzzle pieces all snapping together. The photographer the night we were at

TouTou's. The gray hoodie. Viscount Strathey. The name on the envelope. I jumped off the bed, and Mac made a grab for her computer before it slid to the floor. I snatched the envelope of photographs out of my tote and held them out to her. "It's that kid who was out at the gate the night we went to TouTou's. He took that picture he sent you and he took all these. Look at the name he's using. I think I know what he plans to do."

She looked through them carefully, one at a time. By the time she got to the photograph of the guy who had picked up his pictures at five minutes past noon, making his macho salute with his gun, her face had gone so white I could see individual freckles standing out across her nose.

"Where did you get these?" she whispered.

"He brought them to the photo shop to be developed. We're the only developer within a mile or two of the school. Even still, what are the odds?" I took a breath. "Do you think all that stuff belongs to him? Where did he get it?"

She shook her head. "He's a fast worker, I'll give him that. He hasn't been in the country much over a month, and it had to have taken time to make or buy all this."

The photo in her hand jarred my brain into working again. "Let me see that." It was a picture of a map tacked to a wall over a narrow bed. "Mac, do you know where this is from?"

She shook her head.

"It's from the Spencer Web site. It's a map of the campus." I remembered studying it when Papa had first proposed the boarding-school idea. Drifter's map had been marked up with red X's and circles with "LPG" written inside. There were X's on two sides of each dorm. Inside the library. In the dining room and reception hall. A big blue circle was marked in the center of the field house, and another in the assembly hall where Design Your Dreams was scheduled next month. And there was a red X on Ms. Curzon's office.

"Mac, we've got to tell someone right now. That's why he said that thing about Columbine. That's your blaze of glory." My lungs felt crushed, suffocating me as the full horror of the situation sank in. "He's planning to blow up the school."

"I NEED TO SPEAK to the headmistress immediately." Lady Lindsay Margaret Eithne MacPhail of Strathcairn looked down her aristocratic nose, and I could practically see the glint of a tiara in her red curls.

The principal's assistant, who apparently worked weekends, too, glanced behind her into Ms. Curzon's on-campus apartment, which was on the fourth floor of the administrative wing. "I'm afraid she's out at the moment."

"This is urgent. Would you call her, please, and tell her it's extremely important I see her right away?"

The woman's face set into stubborn lines. "That's not possible. She's having dinner with some members of the board."

"Doesn't she have her mobile with her?"

"Yes, but—"

"Then call her."

"I can't possibly interrupt her meeting for student concerns."

"This isn't a student concern," Mac hissed, her eyes narrowing. "It's about a threat to the school."

"Then you should take it to the director of security."

We had a director of security?

Then I gave myself a mental smack. With the progeny of California's movers and shakers going here, not to mention European royalty and movie stars, of course we did. They must be very discreet, though. I'd never seen as much as a hint of a black suit or a pair of Ray-Bans.

"Fine," Mac said briskly. "Would you call him, please?"

"Mr. Larkin is at home."

"I assume he has a telephone."

"Lady Lindsay, it's Saturday night. The man does take the occasional day off. Would you like to speak to the weekend supervisor?" Was she actually enjoying this?

"This problem is too big to leave in the hands of second-level management such as him or you," she snapped. "I want to speak to the headmistress or Mr. Larkin. If you won't call them, I'll go see them myself. It's urgent. The safety of this whole school is at stake."

The woman—what was her name?—planted her feet in the doorway as though she expected us to rush it. "Before you go interrupting them, how do I know this isn't some kind of prank?"

"Because it's not," I said. "This is real, and it's urgent, and we need Ms. Curzon's help."

"That's what Brett Loyola's older brother said, too, three years ago. Bomb threat, he said. We evacuated the school, called out the bomb squad, and for what? So they could get a free half-day during exams!"

Mac closed her eyes as if she were praying for patience. I felt like doing that myself.

"This is not a prank. It's not exam week. It is serious danger. Now, are you going to help us or not?"

The woman stepped back and swung the door partly shut. "I'll call Natalie when her dinner is over and let her know you two stopped by."

"That's not good enough!" Mac cried. "That's—"

The door closed in her face.

"What kind of idiot gets information about a bomb threat and treats it like this?" Mac raised a fist and moved to bang on the door. I stopped her.

"The kind that thinks all the students are out to make a fool of her." I had to admit that wouldn't be hard to do. "We have to think of something else."

"Someone must have Curzon's mobile number," Mac said. "Or this Larkin man's home phone."

But it was Saturday night and most of the administration had gone home for the weekend.

Mac raised her hand again to bang on the door. "I'll find out what restaurant Curzon's at and we'll go down there."

"She won't tell you."

I proved to be right. The conversation was very short and very rude.

We trooped down the stairs and went back to the dorm wing, having gained nothing but an earful and a demerit each. "The problem is, we don't know when—or even if—this is going to happen," I said. "We don't know where Drif—er, David is."

"But we have proof," Mac said. "We have the picture he sent me of himself that links me to him and we have the envelope of photos linking him to the bombs. If we could just show them to somebody who will believe us, we could get this solved quietly."

"I think the time for quiet is long gone."

"Carly, we are not going to the police. I told you that before. The only reason I agreed to tell Curzon is because she knows how to hush things up."

"Oh, it'll be hushed up, all right. That nasty old bat isn't going to pass on our message and we'll have gotten a demerit for nothing. You just said we have enough proof. The cops will believe us."

"Maybe they will. And if they do, the news crews will be the next to know. And then the entire planet will know that my dad has a psychotic illegitimate son who is targeting me. Can't you just see this on the six o'clock news?"

Consider the alternative: a nice shot of our bodies being loaded into the ambulance in black bags. "It's better than being blown up."

"Easy for you to say. You're nobody."

I sucked in a breath and stopped dead in the middle of the

marble staircase. After all the times she'd hurt me, you'd think I'd be immune to a slap like that.

But I wasn't. Every new wound hurt me just as much, every time.

She put a hand on my arm. "I'm sorry. Carly, I didn't mean that. You're trying to help me and I'm being horrible." She sat on the stairs while I hesitated a step above her, trying to decide if it was safe to be anywhere near her. "I can't seem to help it. It's like a disease."

"Who's got a disease?"

We both looked up to see Lissa, Gillian, and Shani at the top of the stairs, all dressed to go out.

"That's what I'm talking about," I breathed. "Here come the cavalry."

"Don't dare say a word," Mac whispered.

"But—" She shot me a warning glare as we stood up, and I shut up.

"*Zao*, guys." Gillian breezed down the stairs in a cloud of Princess. "What's going on?"

The question of the day. And the answer? At the moment, nothing. Unless I took matters into my own hands. Mac was as stubborn as my little brother, only I didn't have the advantages or size or age to get my way. But we needed help. Five brains had to be better than two—especially when one of them was Gillian's.

Not only that—Lissa has this thing about armies of angels standing at our backs. Well, if ever anyone needed an army, it was me. Right here, right now. *You hear me, angels? Cue formation.*

"Well," I began in a conversational tone, "Mac has a stalker who's not only her secret half brother, but he's also threatening to kill her and blow up the school."

"Carly!" Mac shrieked.

"Curzon and the head security guy are gone and the person

we told doesn't believe us," I went on. "We have proof, but Mac refuses to call the cops."

"Carly! Shut up!"

"So basically we're out of ideas." I gave them all a sunny smile while Mac's face went from dough pale to burning red in seconds. "And how was your day?"

Have you ever seen a redhead lose her temper? Yeah? How about a Scottish redhead? Uh-huh. There's nothing like it. Now I know how William Wallace won all those battles back in the fourteenth century. All that was missing, there on the staircase, was the woad.

It took all four of us to get Mac into our room before Ms. Tobin heard the screaming and dished out more demerits for rowdy behavior. Knowing her, even if we told her what was going on, she'd want to discipline first and ask questions later. In between really amazing Scottish curse words and a few Anglo-Saxon ones I'd heard before, I locked the door and sketched out the rest of the story for the others while they looked through the envelope of photographs and Mac sulked on her bed.

"You took these to Curzon's assistant and she didn't believe you?" Shani asked incredulously. "Are you kidding?"

"She didn't even give us a chance to show them," I said. "Just shunted us off to a guy who isn't here and shut the door in our faces."

"It's nice to know where the students stand," Gillian said. "She'd probably be happy to run a school without all of us underfoot."

"I hope she's *sacked*," Mac said with vicious intensity from behind her seventh or eighth tissue. "Totally irresponsible."

"But what are we going to do?" Lissa said for the fifth time. "We can't just sit here and wait for some lunatic to start planting bombs in the shrubbery."

"There's only one thing *to* do," Gillian replied. "We have to stake out the faculty lot and wait for Curzon to get back. Unless any of you have this Larkin guy's unlisted number."

Of course we didn't.

"Anyone know how to get into the admin offices to find his file? Or hack the employee records in the server?"

I shook my head. "That's your department."

"This is where we could use Lucas Hayes," Lissa said. "At least he would have been good for something."

"I'll take the pipe bombs and the lunatic, thanks," Gillian retorted, and Mac smiled, just a little.

I reached over to touch her hand. "I'm sorry I dished your secret, Mac. But we couldn't do this alone."

"She's right," Shani told her. "No way could you handle this. I'm not even sure we all can handle this."

"We have to do something else." Lissa took one of Mac's hands. "Join hands." Mac looked a little confused as I took the other.

"Father," Lissa began, and I closed my eyes gratefully. "This is an ugly situation and we really need You right now. Please work in David Nelson's heart and make him think twice about hurting anyone. But if he doesn't listen, we pray You'll help us do what's best. Open up people's ears so they'll listen, and lead us to people who will help."

"Amen," I thought I heard Mac say, but I wasn't sure. Gillian said it again, anyway, and we all opened our eyes and took a breath.

And then the phone rang like a fire alarm in the silence.

chapter 16

MAYBE IT'S CURZON." After closing the door in our faces, it was hard to believe her assistant would have given the headmistress our message, but, hey, miracles could happen.

"Or the security guy." Shani walked over to the small table between our beds, where the digital phone sat, but Mac beat her to it.

"Or it's David," she whispered.

"Put it on speaker, whoever it is," I hissed. "And hit the record button to save it to the voice-mail system. All of you, don't make a sound."

Mac activated the recording feature and then pressed the speaker button. If it was Brett calling up from the common room, I was going to be massively embarrassed.

"Yes?" Her tone was lazy and unconcerned, but her face betrayed how stressed she felt.

"Lindsay MacPhail, please," a male voice said. Too young to be the security guy. Too Scots to be anyone at school.

Mac turned white, but her voice stayed level. "This is she."

"Lindsay. Sis. It's David." When she didn't respond, he went on, "Are you alone?"

"Yes."

"No cute little flatmate?"

"She's down in the library, studying."

"On a Saturday night? Poor thing."

"Quite the work ethic," Mac agreed. "But what else can you do when you don't have a date?" She glanced at me and bent her mouth in apology. "But I'm sure you didn't call to talk about my roommate's social life."

"No, I didn't. Take me off the speaker. I want some privacy."

"I'm alone. Isn't that private enough? Besides, I just gave myself a manicure. All my nails are wet and I don't fancy getting Tropical Punch in my hair just so I can talk to you."

He made a rude noise that might have been his way of laughing. "I can't tell you how happy I am that we're finally close to meeting. Have you taken my advice and called your father?"

"Yes."

"And he put you in the picture?"

"Yes."

"So you see why we had to meet."

"No, I don't, actually. I could happily have gone my whole life not knowing you were alive."

"Harsh, little sister. You see, the thing is, I have plans for us."

"The only person who can make plans for me is me."

Shani and I exchanged a glance. The girl had guts.

"Ah, but you're wrong there. Haven't I proven that? I've worked hard to stay in touch and let you know what I was doing every step of the way. Even if you didn't return the favor. Skipping off to America without telling anyone. Tsk, tsk."

"How did you find me?" Mac asked coolly. Guts or not, she gripped the edge of the bed so hard, I half-expected her fingernails to punch through the duvet.

"Let's put it this way. I'm very good with computers, and I have a friend who throws bags at Gatwick. It didn't take much to have him alert me any time your name came up on the manifest. I've been tracking your trips back and forth between London and Edinburgh for some time now."

"You're very thorough."

With our eyes, Gillian and Shani and I agreed: Creepy and sadistic and weird, more like.

"So now I think it's time for us to meet."

"Why? What's the point?"

A second of silence. "Brothers and sisters should know each other. Don't you want to get to know me? What my plans are?"

He actually sounded hurt. I put my hand on the photographs and shook my head. *Don't let him know you know.*

"Not especially."

He sighed. "Lindsay, you've grown up to be a hard woman, just like the countess. She took your dad away from my mum, you know."

"I'm sure he had something to do with the decision. Besides, your mum was married at the time."

"Yeah, to a brute who beat her."

"Look, I'm sorry your mother made bad decisions. I'm sorry you had a rough childhood. But you have to let go of that. It has nothing to do with me."

"I'm making up for lost time. If circumstances had been different, you and I would have grown up together, and I'd be the heir to Strathcairn instead of that nitwit. Your cousin."

"Roger isn't a nitwit. He's very nice. He has a degree in economics from the University of Edinburgh. I'm sure he'll do wonders for the old place."

"Not even a tiny bit jealous?"

"That's none of your business, David."

"Aha, you are. So that gives us one more thing in common. Which brings me to the reason I'm here."

"I don't care what your reasons are. Your life has nothing to do with mine, now, then, or in the future. I'm going to hang up and you're never going to contact me again."

"Or what?"

"Or I'll bring the police down on you for harassment."

He laughed for real this time, and a shivery feeling ran down my back. "Sending e-mail is harassment? I think not, especially when a certain lady puts herself out there on MySpace for anyone to see."

"My school address wasn't on MySpace. I'll report you to the headmistress."

"You'll do nothing of the sort. All you have is some friendly e-mail from a family member. The coppers will just laugh at you, pat you on the head, and send you on your way."

Since this was, in essence, what had already happened, Mac nibbled on her lip and glanced at the envelope of photos. I gripped her wrist and shook my head. *Don't say it.*

"What on earth do you want, then?" she finally asked.

"I want to meet you. Talk face to face. Get to know each other."

"And if I don't want that?"

"Then I'll have to persuade you."

She snorted. "Nothing would induce me to do something that crazy."

"Oh, no? What if something were to happen to your little flat-mate? Or your friends? Or, in fact, your toffy school?"

"What do you mean? Is that a threat?"

"I'm just laying out the consequences if you don't listen to your big brother."

"What consequences, exactly?"

"I'm not prepared to tell you that just yet. I'm keeping it in reserve. So, are you free for dinner?"

"Dinner was ages ago."

"How about a nice little cuppa in an hour, then?"

"No. I don't want to meet you at all." The rising pitch of her voice told us the tension was beginning to get under the lid of Mac's control.

"Lindsay, Lindsay. Don't make me do something drastic. The results will be all your fault."

"They'll be *your* fault, you mean. Your actions have nothing to do with me."

"That's where you're wrong. Meet me in an hour at the Cow Hollow Café, or I won't be responsible for what happens."

"Rubbish."

"All right, then. Don't say I didn't warn you. And, oh, by the way, if you tell anyone about our conversation, I'll know. And those consequences I mentioned? They'll happen whether you meet me or not. So let's keep it between us two."

"You're crazy," she spat.

"Not at all. Sober as a judge. If you change your mind, drop me an e-mail." He hung up without waiting for a reply.

Mac's hand shook so badly she could hardly keep her finger on the disconnect button long enough to silence the dial tone. Then she pressed her fingers to her lips and looked at us all. "He can't be serious. He won't really do anything, will he?"

"There are all those red X's and blue circles," Gillian said slowly. "What if those are where he's going to place the bombs?"

"What if he's done it already?" Shani whispered.

"He can't have." I fished the picture of the map out of the envelope. "Look. One of them is in Ms. Curzon's office, and we know it's locked and empty."

"What about those two by the dorm? What are they?"

Lissa leaned in to look at the map. "That's right outside Vanessa and Dani's room. They're on the ground floor." She stood up. "Be right back."

Less then a minute later, my cell phone rang. Mac jumped about a foot and looked as though she were going to burst into tears. Caller ID said it was Lissa. "Hey. That didn't take long."

"Carly," she said in a whisper, though the likelihood of anyone being in Vanessa's room to hear her on a Saturday night was nil. "You know that picture of the pipes all stacked up?"

I tried to push a word out, but it didn't come. I cleared my throat and tried again. "Yes?"

"I just took a picture with my phone. I'll send it right now."

"A picture of what?"

"A bunch of them are here under Vanessa's window, sitting on the ground."

"ALL RIGHT, HERE'S the plan."

Gillian and Shani were the only ones hanging onto their cool. The rest of us were in hysterics. Mac couldn't stop crying; Lissa had come back as pale as bleached muslin and couldn't even hold a pencil, she was shaking so badly; and I'd already been to the bathroom to . . . well, anyway, I felt better now.

"Lissa and I will go and get someone from Security—anyone, we don't care who—and show them the bombs," Gillian told us. "Shani, you get Curzon's assistant and force her to call Curzon back here. Don't take no for an answer. Mac, you and Carly stay in this room and don't move. The cops will want to talk to you about the e-mail messages and the photographs, and they'll want that recording, too."

"But he said not to tell anyone," Mac protested, her voice wobbly and breaking. "He's watching the school—he'll see the police arriving."

"We'll tell them to go to the field house and take the rain tunnel."

I stared at Shani. "The what?"

"The rain tunnel. You know, to get to the pool and volley-ball courts without getting soaked. You mean you've been going around on the street all this time?"

How many days this past winter had I dashed through the downpour, wondering why on earth the Phys. Ed. facilities were so far away from the main buildings? Rain tunnel. Who knew?

"Stay on topic," Gillian said impatiently. "Even if he is watching, he can't see everywhere at once. Security can check all the red X's inside the building. I don't know what the blue circles are, but they can check those, too. He'll never know."

"Right." Shani, still dressed to kill in a black Dsquared chiffon minidress and red stiletto heels, grabbed her Raven Kauffman evening bag and headed out. Gillian and Lissa followed.

The room seemed huge and empty and a little bit scary once my friends had scattered on their missions.

Mac slid her hand out of mine and walked into the bathroom. I heard splashing and when she came out, she went straight to her wardrobe.

"What are you doing?" I asked. "You don't need to change for the cops."

"I need to wear something practical. These jeans and trainers, yeah? In case I have to bolt?"

I stared at her, my mouth falling open. "What are you talking about?"

Mac's freshly washed face set into white determination. "You heard him. He'll do whatever it is he's going to do if I don't go to that café. He'll do it even if I go. But I have to try talking him out of it."

"You're not seriously thinking about going?!" My heart nearly stopped, then began to pound. "Mac, you can't. He's a lunatic. He'll hurt you."

"If I don't go, he'll hurt a whole lot of other people. You saw those pipe bomb things. They mean serious damage."

"But Security will clean them out."

"I can't risk it. What if the cops take their time getting here? What if Security does nothing but give the girls another demerit? He said an hour, and we've taken up half of that. At least if I go, if I meet him and act like his long-lost sister, maybe I can talk him into calling it off."

"You don't really think he will."

"What I think doesn't matter. I have to try, anyway."

"But what if he does something to you?"

She dragged a pair of sneakers out of the back of the wardrobe. "We'll be in a public place. Besides, I know how to handle myself."

Without another word, I hurried into a pair of Citizens of Humanity cargo pants, snapped up on sale because the bigger sizes always go last.

"What are you doing?" Mac demanded.

"I'm going with you."

"Carly, you can't. He said I was to tell no one. It's all very well for Security to go sneaking about, but if he sees you walk in with me, he'll know I've told."

"He doesn't have to see me." I pulled on a black T-shirt and hunted through my own wardrobe for my jean jacket. "The Cow Hollow Café is a block from where I work. I'll take the bus and double back."

"And do what?"

"Watch out for you. When you get there, call me and then hide your phone in a pocket or something. I'll be able to hear what's going on."

I slipped my wallet and all the money I had on me into my jacket, and dropped my cell phone into a leg pocket, along with my tiny emergency kit containing thread, needles, nail scissors, Band-Aids, Advil, a PowerBar, and a spare lip gloss. It usually lives in my handbag, but I didn't want to have to worry about keeping track of that tonight.

"What if he sees you? What if he recognizes you?"

"He won't." I pulled my hair back in a ponytail and stuffed it through the back of a ratty 'Niners cap I'd lifted from Antony's bureau to get him back for some prank he'd pulled on me. Then I scrubbed off all my makeup. Without that, and without heels and my normal dress-to-impress clothes, I looked about twelve years old. I looked . . . anonymous. Like a thousand other girls that no one would give a second glance as they passed on the street.

"Point taken," Mac said, and grabbed her handbag. "I'll call a cab when we're off the grounds. Let's go."

chapter 17

‹

UNLIKE ME, MAC knew where the entrance to the rain tunnel was: a nondescript door in the corridor behind the dining room. I didn't want to know who had shown it to her. Brett, probably, or Vanessa. I had no doubt the people on the A-list knew every secret passage and unmarked door Spencer Academy could boast. In a place where privacy was at a premium, you'd need to find somewhere for your romantic moments, wouldn't you?

We jogged along the concrete tunnel for what seemed like twenty minutes, emerging next to the boys' changing room by the pool. This meant I'd have to backtrack the long way around the edge of the soccer field to the street where the bus stopped, but at least Mac would be out from under her half brother's surveillance—if he were even watching.

She called a cab from the vestibule of the field house and I leaned on the glass door, my breath fogging it as I whispered to God. "I hope this is the right thing to do, Father," I said softly. "Please go with us. We need Your protection tonight."

The silence in the vestibule made me turn. "Who are you

talking to?" Mac asked as she slipped her phone into an inside pocket in her tweed bomber jacket.

"God," I said simply.

"Again?"

"Just reminding Him we need help."

"Well, I don't suppose it can hurt."

Which, considering her attitude toward anything to do with Christianity, was quite a concession. "Please be careful, Mac," I said. "If something goes wrong, I'll make like I just happened by, and come and join you. Then we'll leave together."

She nodded. "If it's in a public place he can't do anything. I'll be okay. And I'll phone you as soon as I get there."

The cab, which couldn't have been more than a few blocks away, pulled up to the door. Or, more likely, Spencer had the whole company at the students' beck and call.

"Maybe I'll even ask the driver to wait," she said as she got in. "Then we can get out of there together."

"Good plan."

I watched the taillights disappear over the hill, then began to jog down the street to the bus stop. I made it to the corner just in time to see the Muni bus pull away and roar down the hill, blasting diesel exhaust into the atmosphere.

"Wait!" I screamed, running full tilt after it. "Wait for me!"

No luck. "Aughhh!" Why did I have to miss it now, of all times? Clutching my cap in frustration, I debated whether to wait at this stop or walk to the next one—at least I'd be doing something to get myself farther downtown. Meanwhile, Mac was probably already getting out of the cab, thinking I was somewhere close to help her if she needed it.

While I stood on the sidewalk, wavering, a sleek vintage car rumbled up to the curb.

Brett Loyola, driving what looked like a healthy version of my Tío Miguel's 1968 Camaro and looking like he'd stepped out of a magazine, shoved the gear shift into park. He leaned over and rolled the passenger window down.

"Hey, Carly. You okay?"

Any other time I would have been like, *Ooh, he recognized me even in jeans and a ball cap.* Now I just felt a sinking in my stomach. If Brett had spotted me, that meant David could probably recognize me at a glance, too. And our nice little plan would be unusable.

"Sure," I finally said, leaning down to talk through the window since it was clear he wanted an answer and wasn't just being polite. "I'm just waiting for the bus."

"The *bus*?" Had he never heard the word before?

"Some of us don't have cars here." *Some of us don't even have cars.* Surreptitiously, I glanced up the street. *Come on, bus, come on.* Had it been fifteen minutes yet?

"Do you need to go somewhere? I can drop you."

Suddenly he had my full attention. "You can?"

"Sure. Hop in." He pushed open the passenger door and I got in. Fell in, more like. Camaros are very low to the ground.

He flipped an illegal U mid-block and headed down the hill. "Where to?"

"Do you know where Piccadilly Photo is in Cow Hollow?"

"Uh, no. Why would you want to go there at nine o'clock at night?"

I thought fast. "Because it's payday and my boss wants me to pick up my check after he does the reconciliation."

Silence while he tried to stare at me and watch the traffic at the same time.

Carly, as Gillian would say, you've just blown your cover.

Well, guess what. I totally did not care.

Brett shook his head. "Let me get this straight. You work at a photo shop?"

"Yes. Can you go any faster?"

"Not without hitting that guy in front of me."

As it was, we passed the bus a few seconds later, and the bubble of urgency under my breastbone eased a little.

"But why?"

Focused on counting the blocks, I'd lost the thread. "Why what?"

"Why work? And how? Classes and extracurrics and the rowing team wipe out my schedule. Where do you fit a job in?"

"In the slot where the rowing team goes, I guess. I'm not much on team sports."

"But . . . a photo shop? What does that buy you? I can see interning someplace you want to work after college or someplace you can buy stuff, but . . . a photo shop?"

He had clearly never had to hit the sidewalks himself and see exactly how little there was out there for the teenage workforce that didn't involve french fries. "I needed something now."

"What for?"

I took my gaze off the shop fronts long enough to raise my eyebrows at him.

"Sorry. None of my business. It's just not every day that you meet a Spencer kid who does everything and holds down a job, too. I figured there had to be something in it for you."

"A fifteen percent employee discount if I want a digital Nikon or a Sony videocam." We passed the Cow Hollow Café on the left and I pointed to the next corner. Piccadilly Photo's neon sign was still lit, which meant Philip was still there, probably cashing out. "Can you drop me there, please?"

"Oh, no. Curb-to-curb service. Only the best for you."

I gritted my teeth. Since the photo shop was also on our left, it took agonizing seconds for us to go to the next intersection and turn around, then parallel park in front of the shop.

"Thanks, Brett." I pushed on the handle. "I really appreciate this."

"Never stand between a woman and her paycheck," he said cheerfully. "Hey, Carly, before you go . . ."

I had the door open and one foot on the curb. "Yes?"

"Want to go somewhere after?"

"After what?" Come on, come *on*.

"After you get your check. We could catch a movie or something."

You have to be kidding. If you'd asked me this a month ago, I'd have fallen to my knees, weeping in gratitude. But I'm not that girl anymore. "I can't, Brett. I—I have plans. But thanks."

He gave me a girl-melting smile. "I know, lousy timing and no notice. But think about it. Maybe next weekend, okay?"

By which time he would have forgotten this whole little interlude. "Sure. I have to go. Thanks again."

Almost with relief, I swung the car's heavy door shut and dashed toward Piccadilly Photo just as Philip approached the door with his jingly key ring.

"Carly," he said in surprise. "Didn't I say good-bye to you earlier?"

"I'm back." I slipped past him and into the shop. "Philip, I've got trouble and I need your help."

He raised his eyebrows. "A girl in mufti, a Saturday night, and a little derring-do. There's life in the old boy yet. What can I do for you?"

Take that, David Nelson, I thought, and had just enough time to sketch out the important details when my cell phone rang.

CALLER ID SAID it was Shani, not Mac. I tried to calm my galloping heartbeat and answered it.

"Where you parlayin', girl?" she demanded. "You off getting your nails done, or what? You were supposed to stay in the room!"

"I couldn't stop her. Mac's down here at the Cow Hollow

Café, meeting him, and I'm watching her to make sure nothing bad happens."

"I knew you guys wouldn't stay put. Here's the sitch," Shani said, calming down and moving on in her practical way now that there was nothing she could do about it. "Lissa and Gillian freaked. But at least Security's awake now, thanks to the screaming, and the cops are on their way. Whatshername, Curzon's assistant, basically threw me out of the office."

"What is wrong with that woman?" I demanded. "Does she *want* to be blown up?"

"She's been in public administration too long. Anyway, while she was yelling, the name of the restaurant slipped out, but I don't think she realized it. I'm in a cab right now, headed downtown."

"Great. Tell the others what we're doing, but don't call me back. Mac's going to call me and hide her phone while she and David talk, so I can listen. Then we're coming back together."

"Call us as soon as you're safe."

I snapped the phone shut and realized Philip was staring at me with an expression that clearly said, "Can this be real?" By the time I filled in the blanks for him, it had changed to one of those parental looks where you just knew the next words would be, "Go to your room and let me handle this."

"We've already brought the police in," I said, though there wouldn't be anyone in Room 317 to interview at the moment. "Shani is going to get the headmistress, Lissa and Gillian are managing Security, and Mac is at this moment meeting with her half brother, trying to talk him out of whatever he's planning."

"The girl's either recklessly brave or a fool."

Whatever. "The point is, she was supposed to have called me by now so I could listen to them through her phone."

"That's very James Bond of you. But she hasn't called?"

Maybe she couldn't get cell reception down here. Or maybe

he'd surprised her and was already there. "That's where you come in. I want you to take me to the Cow Hollow Café. Pretend to be my *abuelito*—my grandfather. We'll get a table close to them so we can hear what they're saying, and Mac will know she's got friends with her."

He leveled his austere gaze at me. "You know you should wait for the police."

"There isn't *time*." As every second ticked by, something we hadn't planned for or expected could happen to Mac.

"All they need is a bunch of girls galloping about the city, mucking things up."

"Maybe not, but we're all we've got. Don't you see? None of the adults would listen before. We had to do the best we could. Now, are you going to come with me?"

"Hold on." He put a hand on my arm. "You say this boy dropped off his pictures here. He's going to recognize me. I helped him at the counter."

"He might recognize me, too. But we have to risk it. We can't leave Mac in there all alone."

"It would be foolish to risk him knowing she's told someone, all the same. I don't see that you have a choice, unless we settle for loitering on the street."

It hadn't been much of a plan from the beginning. James Bond would laugh—so would Gillian, for that matter. But it was all I had.

Lord, I am way out on a limb here, and I really need Your protection and help. Keep us safe. Help Mac convince David he doesn't have to do this. Give me courage to do what I have to and to recognize Your will when I see it.

Philip looked down at me curiously and I forestalled him. "Don't ask. I'm praying, okay?" He nodded and would have said something else, but at that moment my cell rang again. I sucked in a breath when I saw the display. "It's her."

"Ah." I don't know whether he was responding to the first answer or the second one.

I turned up the volume as far as it would go, and in the quiet of the empty shop, I heard a male voice say, ". . . have that table there, by the tree?"

Someone who must have been the waitress said, "The window table is free. Wouldn't you rather have that?"

"No." There was a bunch of noise and then something clunked, and over that David said, ". . . want to see pictures of it?"

"No, I don't," Mac said impatiently, loud and clear. She must have stashed her phone in a chest pocket. "I want to know that you're not going to do anything to hurt anybody now that I've done what you said."

"If I'd wanted to hurt anybody, I'd have waited until Monday, when everyone is back from the weekend."

Two Scottish accents, yet they sounded completely different. I could hardly understand him. Maybe it was because Mac's enunciation had been ironed smooth in a London school and his was still as rough and scratchy as raw wool.

"So you're not going to do it, then?"

"Do what, exactly?" He paused. "What is a 'bear claw'?"

"It's a pastry."

"Sounds interesting. Are you always this blunt and snappish?"

"Only to people who threaten to blow up my school."

Silence fell, and my blood halted in my veins. He'd never said anything about that in his e-mail messages to her.

"What?"

"Nothing." Ice clinked in a glass.

"What's this about blowing up your school? Who told you that?"

"Nobody."

"What can I get for you?" The waitress's voice again.

"A decaf Ethiopian blend, please, and some carrot cake," Mac said smoothly.

"Okay. And for you?"

"A bear claw."

It sounded so ordinary. At the same time, utterly surreal.

"One carrot cake, one bear claw, two Ethiopians. Cream?"

"No, thank you."

"Sir?"

"No. Go away."

"There's no need to be rude," Mac said. "She's just doing her job."

"I want to know where you got this idea about blowing things up."

"Well, you said something about Columbine." Mac's voice dropped. No wonder. All she needed was for someone to over-hear *this* conversation. "What were you going to do? Go in with a rifle under your raincoat?"

He snorted. "Bit dramatic, aren't you?"

"You should talk."

"Of course not. I'm not a lunatic."

I exchanged a glance with Philip, huddled next to me with one ear trained on the little silver phone. *Riiiiiight.*

"So what's all this about going out in a blaze of glory, then?" Mac wanted to know.

"Oh, that was just to get your attention. I was feeling pretty low that day."

"Well, I'm feeling pretty annoyed," she said, her voice pitched low yet crackling with fury. "And used, and half-tempted to ring the police and turn you in."

"Your own brother, whom you've just met? You wouldn't do that."

"I want your word that, now that we've met, you'll drop all this 'blaze of glory' and 'my days are numbered' crap. How low were you feeling when you wrote that?"

"Did I write that?"

"Yes, and I have the hard copy to prove it. And while we're on the subject, I'd like to know how you got my school address."

"Easy," he said, the ice in his water glass making a singing sound. He must be swirling it around and around. "Your posh school's Web site lists contact names for every department. The convention's the same for all of them. First initial, last name. I typed it in, and when no mailer demon came back telling me it was wrong, I knew I had it. You might have replied, though. What a rude girl you are."

"Of course, stalking isn't rude," she retorted.

"I never stalked you." He sounded offended. "I was reaching out to my only sister. It's not my fault she never bothered to reply."

"Well, I'm replying now. And you still haven't given me your word."

"About what?"

"On the phone, you said if I didn't come down here and meet you, something would happen to my friends or to the school. Now that I'm here, I want your word you won't do whatever it was."

"Don't tell me what to do."

"I'm not." She took a breath, then said more quietly, "I kept my side of the bargain. Now I want to know if you're going to keep yours."

"Are you calling me a liar?"

I caught my breath. *Don't let him bait you, Mac.*

"If something happens, I'll know one way or the other, won't I? So it's up to you."

"All right," he said. "As long as you do what I say, nothing will happen to your friends."

This didn't sound very comforting. I exchanged an anxious glance with Philip, whose face had set in long lines as he listened.

"What do you mean?" Mac asked.

"I want you to come with me."

Ice chinkled as she set her water glass down. "That wasn't in the deal."

"I say what's in the deal or not."

"Here you go." The waitress was back. "Two coffees. I'll be right back with your food."

"Never mind," David said. "We've changed our minds."

"What?" Mac said.

"I want to show you something."

"And I'm not moving. I want my cake."

"That's so like you. To have your cake and eat it, too. Well, that isn't going to work anymore."

"What do you—let go of me!"

"Don't make a scene, little sister." David's voice sounded very close. A door closed in the background, and street noise swelled. "Just like Dad. No mess, no scene. Just pretend we're walking together and everything is lovely."

"Take your hand off me! Mmmf!"

And to my horror, the connection went dead. I shook it and looked at the display.

SIGNAL INTERRUPTED.

chapter 18

"COME ON!"

I dashed out of Piccadilly Photo, dimly aware that Philip had stopped only long enough to lock the door before he walked very fast after me. I ran across the street against the light, causing a minivan to slam on its brakes and honk, and arrived, panting, in front of the Cow Hollow Café.

Mac and David had vanished.

Next to the curb, a taxi started to pull into traffic. I leaped for the door handle and he slammed on the brakes as I wrenched the door open.

"*Señor*, where is the redheaded girl you brought here?" I asked in rapid-fire Spanish. "Didn't she tell you to wait for her?"

The Mexican cabdriver backed his cab out of danger before he leaned over to answer me. "I didn't bring a girl. I got a call to pick someone up here. If you want a ride, get in."

My stomach did a sickening flip-flop. "Was there a cab here when you got here?"

"Why would they call one if there was? Are you my fare or not?"

"No." I didn't know what to do. "No, I guess not."

Philip caught up to me as the cab swerved out into the stream of traffic and fishtailed away. "Was that her? Did we miss them?"

"It's not her cab." I felt like someone had scooped out my insides, leaving me cold and hollow. "I said I'd watch out for her and now she's completely gone."

Even at this time of night, the sidewalks were busy with people window-shopping or sitting outside little cafés like this one, or just strolling and enjoying a spring evening. It could have been the deeps of winter for all I knew. My skin had gone cold, my hands stiff, as I looked up and down the street, desperately searching for a flash of red hair.

"Come on," Philip said. "We can't just stand here. We'll comb the street and meet back here in fifteen minutes."

But we both turned up nothing.

"I don't know what to do," I moaned. "What if he hurts her? It'll be all my fault."

"It will not," Philip contradicted me crisply. "It's this Nelson chap's fault, not yours. There's nothing more we can do here. You need to get back to school and tell the police everything you know."

"Right. You're right." I knew that.

Father, tell me where she is. And please, Lord, keep my friend safe. Put Your foot in front of David and make him trip so she can get away. Something. Anything. Just so we find her, Lord.

Philip flagged down a passing cab and put me into it, even pressing a twenty into my hand for the fare. "Call me as soon as they find her," he said. "I'm going to keep looking. And please be careful."

I sat, stunned and stupid, in the backseat as the cabbie negotiated the first of the hills on the way back to school. How could they have disappeared so fast? They must have gotten into her cab. She wouldn't have sent it away. If she hadn't seen me at the café, she'd have wanted that method of escape.

But what if David had used it against her? What did he want to show her and where was it?

I could only think of one thing, and it frightened me. He'd never really said he wouldn't go ahead and do what he'd threatened to do. Maybe her little slip about blowing up the school had tipped him off that she knew something. And whether she was his sister or not, he had to find a way to keep her quiet.

As far as I knew, David didn't know she'd already told the entire world. That was the only thing we had going for us.

I dug my phone out of my pocket and dialed Gillian.

"Carly, thank heavens," she said. "Tell us what's going on."

"I lost her." My throat closed and I couldn't say a word for a couple of seconds. I tried again. "I went and got Philip and she called me so we could listen to her talking to David. Then he told her he wanted to show her something and they went outside the café, and the signal went dead, and by the time we got there, they were gone." Silence hissed on the line as the cab mounted another hill. "Gillian?"

"I'm still here. I'm thinking. Where are you now?"

"In a cab on the way back to school. Are the cops there?"

"Not yet. But Ms. Curzon arrived with Shani and all you-know-what broke loose."

"At this point, you could tell me we're all going to be suspended and I wouldn't care."

She laughed, and the breath I'd been holding whooshed out of me. "Isn't that the truth? But she'll be looking for a new assistant tomorrow. I'm in the hallway outside your room. Lissa and Shani are in there with her, showing her and the security honcho the pictures and the stuff on Mac's laptop."

"Gillian, where could she go?"

She knew I wasn't talking about the headmistress. "Think it

through. The guy has been here a month. That's long enough to find a place to stay and maybe get a job while he orders bomb parts over the Net. But he isn't going to know San Francisco very well, and he has to use cabs or public transportation, right? So the odds are he's either taken her to his place or they're coming here, to Spencer."

"He said if he really wanted to blow up the school, he'd do it Monday, when everyone's back from the weekend."

"Not good." Gillian thought for a moment. "There was this episode of *CSI* where the bad guy took pictures of his victims and mailed them to their families, and that's how they caught him. He was in front of some car repair place. Can you remember anything from those pictures? Anything that would tell us where he lives?"

I tried to remember the photos I'd stuffed into the envelope.

Envelope.

The envelope!

"Gillian, I wrote his phone number on the envelope. If it's not a cell or a fake, couldn't you find out where he lives from that?"

She gasped. "That's it!"

I heard the sound of a door being wrenched open. "Ms. Curzon! Carly says the guy's phone number is on the envelope. I bet we could find out where he lives on four-one-one-dot-com. Give me that laptop."

I swear, if Gillian doesn't become a forensic scientist, the world is going to miss out.

Keys clicked frantically. "Carly, are you still there?"

"I'm here. We're nearly at the school."

"You're not going to believe this. The number is actually listed. It's not his, though. It's some person named Clyde at 1721 Bautista Court." Clickety-click. "MapQuest says that's about two blocks east of San Francisco State."

"No way." *Lord, do You have something to do with this?* "Maybe he made it up and it belongs to some innocent frat house."

"We can't take the chance. Umph—hey!" I blinked at the sounds of struggle, and then Ms. Curzon came on.

"Miss Aragon, where are you?"

"In a cab, on my way up the hill."

"Good. I want you here in your room, safe and sound, in ten minutes. Is that clear?"

"But, ma'am, we just found out where David may have taken Mac. If they're not already somewhere on campus, that's the only other place they could be."

"Admirable detective work, but nothing to do with you. Members of the San Francisco Police Department have just arrived, and they tell me the FBI are on their way. They want to talk to you rather badly. Ten minutes, understood?"

All kinds of bad things could happen in ten minutes. A fuse could be lit. A finger could tighten on a trigger. "Yes, ma'am." I disconnected the phone and slipped it into my pocket.

Lord, it's me again. What do I do now? Go back to school or try to help Mac?

God? Are You there? Help me.

The cabbie stamped on the accelerator to beat a red light, and we swooped up the second-to-last hill. Below and behind us, the city spread its carpet of lights. Thousands of lights, each marking someone who at that moment had no idea what was going on up here on the hill.

Lights spread out behind me.

Like Lissa's armies of angels, spread out at her back.

At mine, too. Those angels were fighting on my side. But I had to lead the way. All it would take was one courageous step forward. I tamped down the swarm of dipping and swooping butterflies in my stomach and tapped the driver on the shoulder.

"Change of plans. Take me to 1721 Bautista Court."

❦

THE HOUSE WAS nothing special. It might have been built when my grandparents were young—and it hadn't had much in the way of upkeep since. I asked the driver to go past it and park around the corner.

"You want me to wait, miss?" He eyed the deserted street.

"Would you mind? Just stay out of sight."

"Are you in some kind of trouble?"

Gee, did it show? Maybe the fact that I was as jumpy as a bean on a hot stove gave it away. "No, but my friend is. She's with a—an abusive relative and I'm trying to do an intervention."

He nodded. "My cousin did one of those. Got his daughter into rehab. You shouldn't do that alone. Want me to help?"

Thanks, Lord, for bringing me this guy instead of the last driver. "That's okay. Just be ready to drive away really fast if I can get her away from him."

"I can do that." He settled behind the wheel. "Mario Andretti ain't got nothing on me."

I ignored the fact that I had nothing on me to pay him with except Philip's twenty, and the meter had left that behind a while ago. First things first: Mac, then the cabbie.

My phone twittered, telling me I had a text message.

TEXT MESSAGE

Natalie Curzon   Where are you? Return immediately or face consequences.

There would be consequences if I left now, and they would be way more urgent. I set the phone to vibrate and put it back in my pocket. The street was silent—one of those old residential neighborhoods with hedges and trees and a tiny Chinese market on the corner. The rumble of an engine cruising up behind me very slowly sounded loud enough to wake the dead.

Too loud. Too slow. *Be aware of your surroundings.*

My heart kicked into gear and I whirled as the vintage Camaro growled to a stop at the curb. The engine shut off and Brett got out.

I gawked at him like a total nimrod. First we couldn't find help to save our lives, and now help was practically falling out of the sky. What was up with that?

"What are you doing here?" I squeaked in a voice so high it was practically a whisper.

"You're in trouble, aren't you?" He took my arm and led me over to the passenger side. "Relax, I'm not going to kidnap you. I just don't want to talk out here on the street."

At least it was dark inside the car, so he couldn't see my face. My mouth was still hanging open and I couldn't seem to say anything more coherent than "What—what—?"

"I followed you," he said simply, making himself comfortable behind the wheel. "I was parking my ride when I saw you go past in the cab. Then two seconds later I saw him do a U-ball and take off with you. My weird-o-meter started buzzing, so I followed, and here I am." He looked up and down the street. "Is everything okay?"

My brain tried to process these facts. *Brett saw you in the cab. He thought you needed help. He drove all the way across town on the off chance that you weren't just going to get a box of tampons.*

What did this mean?

"Are you having a slow night?" I blurted. "I mean, don't you have anything better to do than follow people around town and offer them rides?"

His face crumpled in confusion, then smoothed out as pride got the upper hand. "I thought you might need help." He put the keys back in the ignition and even in the silver light of the street lamp, I could see his face had suffused with color. "But, hey, you know, if you're just going to see a friend and I'm butting in, I can go. Sorry."

"No, wait." What was the matter with me? Fear had obviously unhinged my brain. "I'm the one who's sorry. And, yes, I do need help. Mac's been kidnapped by her illegitimate half brother, who we think has planted bombs all over the campus and plans to blow it up on Monday morning, if he doesn't do it tonight."

Brett dropped the keys, and spent the next thirty seconds fishing them out from under his own feet.

While he did that, I explained.

"And so that's when I told the cabbie to turn around, because the phone number on the envelope was registered to 1721 Bautista. There's a fifty-fifty chance that David actually lives in that house there with the shrubs out front, and an even lower one that he brought her back here."

"To do what?"

I shook my head. "He said he wanted to show her something, but in his e-mail messages he said crazy stuff like her days were numbered and they were going out in a blaze of glory. That doesn't sound good to me."

"Not exactly an offer for soda and a pizza," he agreed. Number 1721 was three houses down, and he gazed at it, his eyes flicking from porch to sidewalk to windows. "What's the plan?"

"You're assuming I have one."

"You're here, aren't you? That means you were going to do something, all by yourself."

"I hadn't gotten that far." I followed his gaze to the house. "It doesn't look like anyone is home, does it?"

"Doesn't mean anything. He could just be keeping the lights off. Why don't I go see if he'll answer the door?"

I stared at him. "Are you nuts? He knows who you are."

"What?"

"He's been stalking her for weeks. He saw us all go to that party at Callum's, and he even knows what time you and Mac came back." Even though I was totally over him, I felt the blood creep into my face.

"And what time was that?"

I shrugged. "Sometime after three, I guess. Not that I was, um, watching the time or anything."

"Then it wasn't me. I left after you did." His gaze flicked to me. "The party lost some of its juice when you took off."

I snorted. "Yeah, right."

"For me, it did."

Had I heard that right? His voice was kind of muffled. It must have been a mistake. I hurried on. "Anyway, he told her she couldn't tell anyone, so if you show up on the doorstep, he'll know she did and he might hurt her. Drive around to the next street, okay? Let's look at the back of the house."

The darned Camaro sounded like a Harley without a muffler. Did Mac know Brett drove this monster? Would she recognize the sound and know that the cavalry was on its way?

We rumbled around the corner and I leaned out of the window long enough to wave at the cabbie and tell him I'd met a friend. Brett loaned me another twenty and the cab sped away, the nice cabbie waving out his window, leaving the two of us on the street behind the house.

"Come on." I waited for him to lock up and we ran down the driveway of a nondescript duplex where someone inside was watching TV, the blue light flickering on the drapes. Behind the garage was a chain-link fence, and I thanked God for Mac's foresight on the subject of footwear.

Brett and I dropped as soundlessly as the jingly fence would let us into the backyard of number 1721. "Now what?" he whispered. "This is trespassing. Are we going to break in next?"

Is my life full of weirdness or what? Here I was, sneaking through the undergrowth, trying to pull off a nocturnal rescue and contemplating criminal acts with Brett Loyola, scion of one of San Francisco's wealthiest families. I swear, you can't make this stuff up.

In the pocket of my cargo pants, my phone vibrated against my leg like an angry cicada. I ignored it. "This is a multi-unit house," I whispered, scanning the back of the building. "It's just like the ones on my Tía Donna's street, only uglier. The family lives on the main floor and rent out the separate suites upstairs."

"So that's where you think he's got her? In one of the upstairs apartments?"

I shook my head. How should I know?

There was a rush of movement in the yard next door, and a big dog flung itself at the fence, barking. I grabbed Brett's arm and threw myself on the ground behind a group of plants in huge ceramic pots at the edge of the patio.

Lights came on next door, and someone called the dog in.

Lights came on above us, too. The right-hand suite, overlooking the back deck. For two seconds, I saw a head silhouetted against the window, red hair tousled and the face a pale oval shape.

Someone grabbed her from behind and wrestled her away from the window. The lights went out.

I turned my head and looked at Brett, on his knees next to me, both of us with gravel mashed into our jeans and the palms of our hands. The scent of rosemary hung in the air. I realized a second later that it came from the thick, prickly bushes growing in the pots, which did a great job of hiding us.

"There's your answer," I said. "Now the only thing we have to decide is who's going up there to get her."

chapter 19

"D ID ANYONE EVER tell you that you are insanely off the hook?"

"Not lately." Nothing moved behind that window. Had David left Mac in there or moved her to a different room? And did she realize that she wasn't alone anymore? "Not ever, actually."

"You know what Vanessa calls you?"

"Besides MexiDog?" My tone sounded bitter. "I don't need to know, thanks."

"MexiDog?" His voice dropped in shock. "That's harsh."

I shrugged. "Can we stay on topic, please?"

"She calls you 'sweet lamb.'" Ew. On the whole, I think I preferred MexiDog. "Because you're so nice to everyone."

"She only says that to stay on Mac's good side," I told him. "Hey, I just thought of something. Do you work on your car yourself?"

"My dad and I do. Why? What's that got to do with anything?"

"Because if you were just a dumb rich kid who didn't know anything about engines, my idea wouldn't be any good."

"Thanks. I think. What's your idea?"

"Go and do something minor to the engine, and push the car down the block so it stops in front of the house. Ask to use the phone or something, but I'm betting that a guy who's handy enough to build bombs wouldn't be able to resist getting his hands on it."

"I thought you said he'd recognize me."

"We have to risk it. If he does, say you were coming to visit your brother in the frat house."

"My brother goes to Stanford."

"Brett." I gave him a look. "This is called extemporaneous acting."

"Okay. I can do that. What are you going to do?"

"Get Mac's attention and get her down from there."

"How long do you want me to stall him?"

I pulled out my phone. "Give me your number and set your phone to vibrate. I'll call you when we're back over the fence."

"What if you run into trouble?" I'd always thought his eyes were amazing . . . long-lashed and dark and penetrating. But now, in the dim silver light of the streetlights behind us, I saw something that made them even more beautiful.

Respect. And concern.

For me.

I shook myself so I wouldn't just fall into his arms like ninety percent of girls probably did. "The police have to be on their way, especially since I didn't turn up at school. We could wait for them, but I'm afraid if he hears them coming and gets scared, he'll do something to her. Brett," I said, putting a hand on his arm, "I don't have a Plan B. This has to work."

"Good enough. Give me your number and I'll buzz you when I'm out front."

We programmed our numbers into each other's phones while the little fangirl inside me did cartwheels and ignored the fact that if it weren't for this crisis, his having my number was the last thing that would ever happen on this earth. Possibly just ahead of the apocalypse.

He raised his head and did a fast recon of the backyard, making sure no one was moving inside the house. Then, he took my chin in his hand.

And kissed me, hard, on the mouth.

My eyes and lips formed three circles of astonishment as he let me go. I'm sure I looked like some stupid cartoon character, because he grinned and whispered, "For luck."

And then he ran into the dark.

I heard the fence jingle softly as he went up and over it, and still I sat there like a melting truffle, touching my lips and wondering if I was dreaming.

Don't wake me up. If this is a dream, maybe it will happen again.

A piece of gravel gouged my knee extra-hard and I winced and snapped out of it. I picked it out of my jeans and then bounced it in my hand as I considered the window.

Not yet.

Out front, I heard a creak like the door of a Halloween house as it swings open to welcome you to your doom. What on earth . . . ? And then I identified it. The Camaro's hood going up. My phone buzzed against my thigh. Not Ms. Curzon—Brett. I silenced it and heard voices out front. I couldn't hear much more than tones, but they were male tones. Two of them.

I tossed the bit of gravel up, softly.

Not hard enough. I picked up another little stone and lobbed it up again, harder. It bounced off the glass with a click.

Nothing.

I threw two bits of stone, then three, and then I started to get scared. What if he'd moved her? What if I were chucking rocks at an empty room, wasting time and maybe even putting Brett in danger for nothing? What if David had that gun tucked into his waistband? What if he recognized Brett and shot him, right there on the street?

My lungs began to constrict and I scooped up a whole handful of gravel. I stood up and flung it at the window in a desperate overhand. Gravel rained down everywhere, pattering on the patio and the drainpipes.

And Mac's face bobbed into view behind the glass.

I waved frantically.

Why was she shaking her head? What was wrong? Why didn't she—

And then I saw the dark strip across her mouth and the strange set of her shoulders. Too straight. Pulled back.

Duct tape. Her hands are taped behind her.

Her feet probably were, too, which was why she'd hopped to the window. At least she wasn't tied to a chair.

I had to get her out of there, and I only had brief minutes. But I hadn't babysat Antony and our yelling horde of semi-cousins for years without learning something. I wrapped my hands around the ivy-covered deck post as high as I could reach, and began to shinny up it. I gained the deck rail just as the lights went on downstairs, illuminating the patio where I'd just been hiding.

I yanked my dangling feet up and out of sight and froze.

Thirty awful seconds went by while someone slid the glass door back and looked outside. Then it slid shut again and the light went out.

The roof extended past the deck rail. I crawled onto it. Then, trying to keep my steps soundless, pulled myself up next to Mac's window.

Her face floated behind the glass, eyes wide and staring above the strip of thick tape. The same tape that had no doubt been used to plug the ends of the pipe bombs.

Fear flip-flopped in my stomach as I tried the window. It slid up. People never locked their second-floor windows. "Mac, are you okay? Did he hurt you?" I whispered.

She shook her head, and tears overflowed her eyes, running silently down her cheeks to be diverted horizontally by the tape.

"This is going to hurt. I'm sorry."

Papa always pulled Band-Aids off us in one fast rip. Now I understood how he must have felt. Mac sucked in a gust of breath through her nose as the tape came off, and she clamped her lips together to keep from crying out.

"I can't get in the window," I whispered. "It's too high and I'll make too much noise. Put your hands up here so I can get the tape off them."

She shook her head. They were tied behind her.

"Bring them to the front. Lie on the bed and slide them under you. Pretend you're a gymnast. Hurry."

It must have hurt, stretching muscles that weren't meant to go in that direction. But she did it, silently. When she rested her hands on the windowsill, she was flushed and breathing hard. But neither of us said a word as I got out my nail scissors and snipped. We pulled and wriggled, and I even used my teeth until the wretched tape came free.

When she'd snipped her feet free, she pulled herself over the sill and out the window. "Thank God," she breathed as she practically fell into my arms. "I didn't think He would listen to me, but you came."

"Me and the angels. Come on. Don't make a sound."

I don't know how we got down off that roof without killing ourselves or bringing the person who lived downstairs outside, screaming about burglars. I remember the dark herbal smell of torn ivy. The grit on the shingles that saved us from sliding down the pitch of the roof. The massive sliver I got in the pad of my thumb when I transferred from the deck railing to wrap my legs around the post that held it up.

And then the scent of rosemary that meant freedom—and Brett's kiss. Even now, when I pass a clump of it in someone's garden, that night comes back to me and I'm right there, kneeling behind those pots in the dark with Brett's mouth on mine.

I went over the back fence a lot more clumsily than the first time, thanks to the sliver and my wobbly knees and trying to help Mac. I thought the racket would bring the whole neighborhood down on us, but they must have been absorbed in the eleven o'clock news, because nothing moved as we slipped down the driveway and back out to the street.

I scrolled to Brett's number and called, then put the phone back in my pocket when it went to voice mail.

Far away, like maybe a mile, I heard the sound of a siren. Two. Then three.

"Carly, where are we?" Mac said breathlessly, rubbing her bare arms. She'd begun the evening with a jacket and handbag, and now both were gone. "We have to get out of sight. He'll find us."

Somebody gunned the Camaro into sudden, rumbling life.

She jumped about six inches at the sound and I grabbed her arm. "That's Brett. That's why David left you alone. Brett pretended to have car trouble and knocked on the door."

"Brett?" She sounded dazed. "Brett who?"

"Loyola. Don't run. He'll be here any second."

"From school? That Brett? What does he have to do with any of this?"

"He followed me over here. Listen, it's a long story and I'll tell you everything later." I tracked the sound of the engine to the corner and the short side of the block. The volume of the sirens was increasing, too—in decibels and number.

The Camaro shot around the corner, fishtailed, and straightened as Brett got control of it. Half a dozen police cars, lights blazing like a Boys Like Girls concert, flashed past in the opposite direction and lit up the night sky over the roofs of the houses behind us. Brett pulled up to the curb in a cloud of exhaust and noise.

"Get in!" he shouted, and yanked the passenger seat forward.

Mac dove into the back and I fell into the front, and before I could even get the door closed, he gunned the engine again. I wrestled it closed as we peeled away from the curb.

"What happened?" I said breathlessly, buckling up as fast as my shaking fingers would let me.

"That guy is a total nutcase." His eyes were black with adrenaline and excitement, but his hands were sure on the wheel. "Is Mac okay?"

"I'm fine." Her voice sounded muffled. "Wretched seatbelt. Where is it?"

"Down the side. Lap belt." He rounded the corner and I suddenly realized what he was doing.

"Where are you going?" I demanded. "Get us out of here!"

"They all think Mac's in there, about to be blown up or killed. We need to let them know she's safe."

"No!" Mac grabbed the back of his seat and her voice spiraled into panic. "Get me away from him, now!"

Ahead of us, two police cars blocked the street. Four more were parked helter-skelter on the road and even up on the sidewalk in front of number 1721. As we watched, two uniformed cops ran up the old-fashioned, wide stairs and into the house, while another one pounded up an outside staircase.

And then the entire left side of the house exploded.

Fire and plumes of smoke arced into the air, and the cop on the stairs tumbled all the way down, his arms and legs cartwheeling like those of a rag doll tossed aside by a child.

Wood and shingles and bits of plumbing rained down on the police cars. Fire roared up out of the hole in the roof and, seconds later, the two cops reappeared, staggering with shock, carrying an old man between them who was wearing nothing but a red-splattered robe and a pair of boxers. I wondered, stunned, if that had been who had opened the door while I was climbing up the deck post.

"Brett!" Mac pounded on his shoulder, her fist smacking him so hard I could hear it even through the noise. "The ambulance is coming. We're going to be trapped here if you don't get moving!"

"But they'll think you're—"

"Move!"

He dropped the Camaro into reverse and shot backward, all the way to the corner. Mac rocked forward, then back, and finally found her seatbelt. Just in time, too. He took off like a bat out of you-know-where and headed for the fastest route back to Spencer.

I didn't dare look at the speedometer. Instead, I pulled out my cell phone.

PEOPLE V. DAVID BRANDON NELSON
EMERGENCY SERVICES TRANSCRIPT
MASTER 27, SIDE 2
23:27:04 2009-MAY-02

911 OPERATOR: 9-1-1. What is your emergency?

U/F: My name is Carolina Aragon, and
                I need to tell someone that Lady
                Lindsay MacPhail is safe.

911 OPERATOR: What is your location, ma'am?

ARAGON: We're in the car, heading back to
                school. [Pause] Spencer Academy.
                Lady Lindsay was kidnapped a cou-
                ple of hours ago by her insane half
                brother—

U/F #2:	Carly! Don't tell them that, you idiot!
ARAGON:	—and a whole bunch of cop cars showed up at his house a minute ago, and there was this big explosion, and we're afraid people might think she got blown up, too, but she didn't. We're all safe. Could you let them know that, please?
911 OPERATOR:	Where was this explosion?
ARAGON:	At 1721 Bautista Court. He taped her hands and feet and kept her in the upstairs apartment, but we got her out before it blew up.
911 OPERATOR:	Can you hold the line a moment, ma'am?
ARAGON:	Sure. But I'm down to two bars, so I can't hold for long.
911 OPERATOR:	Stand by, please.
U/M:	SFPD Communications, Sergeant Lombard.
911 OPERATOR:	SFPD, this is 9-1-1. Do you have an incident at 1721 Bautista Court? An explosion connected with a suspected kidnapping?
LOMBARD:	Affirmative. FBI, ambulance, and fire also at the scene. Not to mention some guy from the British Embassy. It's ugly. Possible multiple fatalities.
911 OPERATOR:	Please relay a message to the first responders. Lady Lindsay MacPhail is safe. Repeat, she is safe and in

	the company of unknown persons, apparently on her way back to school.
LOMBARD:	Unknown persons?
911 OPERATOR:	Students, from the sound of it.
LOMBARD:	Confirmed. Will advise.
911 OPERATOR:	Ms. Aragon?
ARAGON:	I'm here.
911 OPERATOR:	Your message has been relayed.
ARAGON:	Oh, thank you. Thanks a lot.
911 OPERATOR:	Do you need assistance? Can I do anything else for you?
ARAGON:	[Pause.] You could try explaining this to my headmistress.

END 23:28:19 2009-MAY-02

chapter 20

I N OUR ABSENCE, Spencer Academy had been evacuated. Not that this was as complicated as it could have been, since it was Saturday night. The day students were at home, tucked in their beds (okay, so that's a little optimistic), and the usual crowd of boarding students had taken off to go surfing at Santa Cruz or rock-climbing at Yosemite for the weekend.

The rest of the student body, which numbered nearly two hundred, had been sent downtown in limos to rough it at the Four Seasons. All, that is, except Shani, Lissa, Gillian, Mac, Brett, and me, who had been loaded into three police cruisers and taken to Brett's parents' place, presumably for safekeeping.

This *must* be the apocalypse.

That's the only explanation I had for a night that, aside from the kidnapping and explosions, had included The Kiss, three rides in the Camaro, and a sleep under the same roof as Brett. Frankly, if the world was really coming to an end, I was good with it. It just wasn't gonna get any better than this.

Brett's parents waited for us at the door of their three-story

renovated Edwardian with its bazillion-dollar view of San Francisco Bay and the Golden Gate Bridge, lit up even at this time
of night. The cop who seemed to be in charge flashed his ID and
made sure we were safely inside before he spoke.

"Sergeant Mason. We'll need to interview the kids in the morning, Mrs. Loyola. We'll be back around ten. Is that all right?"

She took one look at our wan but totally wired expressions
and said, "Better make it noon. I'll make pancakes and frittata
for everyone, including you and your officers, Sergeant."

"That's very kind of you, ma'am, but it isn't necessary."

"I'm feeding everyone anyway, so you're most welcome. We'll
see you tomorrow."

She shepherded us inside and gave us very momlike hugs
as she divided us up into the various bedrooms on the top two
floors. There were a lot of them. There were also silk draperies
imported from Italy, terra-cotta pots filled with orchids and trail-
ing vines, cool tiles underfoot, and—ohmigosh, was that a real
Monet hanging there in the drawing room?

Suffering from a combination of sensory overload and adrenaline high, I wasn't sure I'd be able to sleep. The room Brett's
mother showed me into was somewhere on the second floor, but
I couldn't see anything through its windows. Maybe it faced into
the hillside. Fine with me. I'd had enough of feeling exposed to
last me the rest of my life.

I got into my tank and pajama bottoms, which I'd stuffed into
a tote during the ten minutes they'd given us to get up to our
dorm rooms and pack an overnight bag. I was just climbing into
bed when there was a tap at the door.

"You're not seriously going to bed," Shani whispered when I
opened it. "Come on. You and Mac gotta give us the scoop."

I followed her down the corridor and up a flight of stairs to a
big bedroom with two double beds in it, done up in a pretty English chintz. Draped all over the beds were my friends—minus

Brett, of course. I wondered which room was his—and if I'd see him in the morning.

"She was in *bed*," Shani reported, making herself comfortable in the matching easy chair and tucking her feet up under her. "With all of us up here dying to know what happened."

"All right, spill," Gillian told me, lounging on the other bed next to Lissa. I sat at the bottom of Mac's, where she was leaning on pillows piled against the wrought-iron headboard, the covers pulled right up to her chin. "Start from the moment Lissa and I left to go get Security."

Thinking back past The Kiss and the explosion—what had happened to that old guy in the robe?—seemed like going back into ancient history. Like I'd passed some kind of major milestone and now there was Before and After.

I looked at Mac. "Sure you don't want to do this? You're the one it actually happened to."

"You do the first bit," she said. "And Shani can tell us how she got Ms. Curzon back here. Maybe by then I'll have my head round it all."

So. Before.

"Well, once you guys left, Mac felt it was too risky to not go meet David. We had no idea whether he'd really stand by what he said and blow something up if she didn't show. And of course I wouldn't let her go by herself, so she took a cab to town and I, well, I missed the bus."

Moments too late, I realized I should have glossed over this part. But then, everyone knew how we'd gotten back to school. There was no keeping Brett out of the story.

"Did you?" Mac said. "Then how did—"

"Brett saw me and gave me a ride."

"Aha," Lissa said with satisfaction. "Now it all makes sense."

"I'd like to know how we got from giving Carly a ride to all of us being invited to stay at his house like the best buds we are,"

Shani added. Sarcastic much? "Seems to me there's something really interesting missing out of the middle." Eyebrows raised in two delicately plucked arches, she gave me an expectant look.

"That has nothing to do with what happened to Mac," I said, and they started to laugh. But since I was trying to keep a straight face, too, it was the good kind of laughter. The kind that feels best when you share it.

"So we got down to the Cow Hollow Café and Brett dropped me off at Piccadilly Photo."

"Where?" Lissa said. "What's that got to do with anything?"

I realized that, except for Mac, none of them knew. Wow. Only a day or two ago, keeping my secret had meant everything. Now it was just another footnote in the story. "That's where I work. I told Brett I needed to pick up my check, which was a total lie, and once he left, I asked my boss for help."

"Where you work," Shani repeated.

"You work?" Gillian echoed. "As in, you have a job?"

"Where do you think she got those photographs?" Mac asked them. "Off the Net?"

"Something like that," Gillian said. "And here, all this time, we thought you were having a secret, torrid affair with someone. It never crossed our minds you had a *job*."

"Sad but true. So what happened was—"

"I think she might be now," Shani inserted slyly. "Having a torrid affair, I mean."

"What *happened* was, I developed the pictures myself." She was implying a question I totally didn't know the answer to. "That's what triggered this whole thing. I saw the bombs and stuff, and even though I thought I was wrong or overreacting or crazy, I made an extra set of photos. So when Mac showed me the JPEG attached to the e-mail David sent, I realized her stalker and the guy with the bombs were one and the same person." They glanced at each other, and I took the opportunity to move on. "So, anyway, Mac called my cell secretly when David showed up, so Philip and I could listen in on what they were saying. The problem is, my stupid cell lost the signal, so when they left I had no idea where they went."

"Back to his house," Mac said. "Thanks a lot—I thought you were following me the whole time. I'm glad I didn't know you weren't. I'd have been even more terrified."

"We did, eventually," Gillian said. "Carly had the brilliant idea for me to check the phone number on the envelope on four-one-one-dot-com."

"Except it was registered to some guy name Clyde. We were kind of running blind there. It could have been a frat house or a fake," I said.

Mac shook her head. "David didn't have a phone. That poor old fossil downstairs took his messages for him."

"Criminals can be so dumb." Lissa shook her head. "Who takes pictures of bombs, anyway? And then takes them to a photo shop to be developed? Hasn't he heard of digital cameras?"

"And then wouldn't you put a fake number on your film envelope, anyway?" Gillian wanted to know.

"I'm glad he didn't," Mac pointed out dryly.

Shani took up the story. "By that time, I'd gotten back with Ms. Curzon, after totally interrupting her dinner with the board members and causing a *teensy* little scene in the restaurant." She hugged her knees, smug satisfaction written all over her. I'd have bought a ticket to watch *that*. "It took about six seconds for her to fire her assistant once she got back."

"I should hope so," Mac said. "Idiot."

"I've never seen Curzon like that," Lissa said, her eyes going round at the memory. "She was like a human hurricane. She tore into the security guy, ripped a bunch of skin off him, and the whole department all scattered with copies of David's map to search the grounds. Then she found out you guys were gone."

Lissa shook a hand as if she'd burned it. "Man. She was crazed. Livid. *Molten*."

"At which point the cops arrived to take the brunt of it," Gillian went on. "And then the FBI got involved because it was a kidnap case, and *they* called the British Embassy because *apparently* Mac is a VIP."

"Rubbish," Mac said with a snort, lady that she is.

"Not according to the feds. Curzon had some kind of security agreement to protect you, except that somehow you gave them the slip."

"The rain tunnel," I said, looking at Shani. "Thanks for that."

"Any time," she said. "Glad to help."

"Meantime, after Gillian got me the address, I took a cab over there and Brett found me. Again."

"What, have you got a stalker now, too?" Lissa wanted to know. "This is the part where we get the details, girlfriend."

"We snuck into the backyard and hid behind some big pots and decided that Brett would make a distraction out front while I climbed up and got Mac out of the room she was in. It was obvious she couldn't do it on her own."

"Tied up hand and foot," Mac added. "Took a bit of doing, getting out of it."

"But how did he tie you up in the first place?" Lissa wanted to know. "Don't get me wrong, but I can't imagine you doing anything you didn't want to."

"Thank you." Mac smiled at Lissa, and for the first time, the light was right and I noticed the bruise darkening the skin at her temple.

"Oh, Mac, he hit you," I breathed. "You should have told the EMT guy."

She shook her head. "I've had enough fussing, thank you. Anyway, that part came later, when David finally got that I didn't want to be his sister, didn't want a lovely family reunion at

Strathcairn, didn't want to see him ever again in my life. In fact, I think I told him I'd prefer it if he were dead." She frowned. "Possibly not the smartest thing to say, because really, the poor boy was pathetic. Anyway, at that point he swung at me and I didn't get out of the way fast enough."

Lissa covered her mouth in horror and I reached over to give Mac's foot a supportive squeeze through the covers. To my surprise, she didn't jerk it away. Instead, she smiled at me. It had to be a record for her—three smiles in a row. Real ones.

"While he taped my hands together, he oh-so-kindly told me about the bomb he'd made that was just for the two of us," she went on. "Somehow I think that even if I'd agreed to the slow-motion reunion between father and children in a sunlit meadow, he'd have still done what he did. At that point, that poor dear Clyde man creaked up and told David there was someone at the door and would he help him." She glanced at me. "As soon as he was out of the room, I heard rocks hitting the window. Carly got me out, we did a Spider-Man impression going down the side of the veranda, and next thing I knew, I was being tossed headfirst into Brett Loyola's incredibly noisy car." She laughed. "And the funny thing was, the whole night was so surreal that his turning up seemed quite normal."

"I still want to get to the interesting part between him showing up and him inviting us all to refugee at his house," Shani put in. "Carly, you're leaving something out."

Hot blood crept into my cheeks. "I am not. That's exactly what happened."

"Come on, Carly," Gillian said. "True confessions."

"Leave her alone, you lot." Mac took in the color of my face. "A woman's entitled to her secrets."

"Not this woman. Not the kind of secrets she's been keeping from us all term," Shani retorted. "A job, for heaven's sake. Showing up in the middle of the night with one of the most popular guys in school. Next you'll be telling us you landed a guest spot on VH1."

"No, but I might get a summer job with Tori Wu."

Gillian shrieked and Lissa clapped her hands and pandemonium broke out just long enough for me to hope that they'd all forgotten Shani's question.

But no.

"Congratulations, Carly," Shani said. "But I notice you cleverly did not tell us what we want to know."

I gave up. They'd nag until dawn unless I told. "While we were coming up with the plan in the backyard, Brett kissed me. Is that what you want to know? Are you happy now?"

"Kissed you?" Shani leaned forward. "A real kiss? Or an ohmigosh-we're-going-to-die-good-bye kiss on the cheek?"

"A real kiss. Full frontal. On the lips."

More pandemonium. I swear, at this rate Mrs. Loyola would be calling the cops and *begging* them to take us down to the station.

"So are you guys, like, official?" Lissa wanted to know. "A couple?"

"How could they not be, after this?" Mac asked. "Facing danger, rescuing the damsel, the whole lot. It's destiny."

"It is not, you guys," I mumbled. "It was the heat of the moment. He was just being gallant."

Now Shani snorted through her nose. Such elegance my friends have. "Gallant is holding open the gym door so it doesn't smack you in the face. Cruising up just in time so you don't have to rescue your friend from the insane psycho by yourself is lo-o-o-ve."

"He really followed you over there?" Gillian wanted to know.

I nodded. "He saw me in the cab, right after Ms. Curzon ordered me back to the school. He thought it was weird or that I was in trouble or something. I don't care. I'm just glad."

"I think there was more to it than that," Gillian said thoughtfully.

"Don't say the L word," I begged her. "That's not true, and besides, it's embarrassing."

"It *was* the L word." Gillian smiled at me. "*L* for 'Lord.'"

Lissa nodded slowly. "She's right. Don't you see? God was in on it from the beginning."

"Oh, come on." Mac's voice would have been rough with scorn if she hadn't been so tired and riding the same adrenaline crash I was. "That's a bit presumptuous, don't you think?"

"No." Gillian looked over at me. "God is all wrapped up in the smallest details of our lives. You prayed for help, didn't you." It was a statement, not a question.

I nodded. "Like crazy. I prayed for protection for Mac and courage for myself. Repeatedly."

"And I'd say those were both answered, wouldn't you?" Gillian's face had relaxed into happiness and a kind of awe.

"I don't buy it," Mac said flatly. "You lot are reading too much into it."

"You know that's not true, Mac." The more I thought about it, the more amazing the whole night became. "I mean, I'm not exactly the Spider-Man type, am I? No hero. Just a Latina scholarship kid with a part-time job to finance some fabric for a dress. And there I was, shimmying up that veranda to get you out of that house as if I did spy operations for a living."

"Wait. Whoa." Gillian held up a hand. "That's why you have a job? You're here on a scholarship?"

I nodded. The last of my secrets, thrown out there in the open for my friends to see. It just seemed right to tell them everything, to get it all out, so I could leave Before behind and move on to After. "My father can't afford the tuition to Spencer. I got a full ride. And no one could pay for the fabric for the dress I want to make for Design Your Dreams, so I decided I would. People can laugh if they want." I shrugged. "I'm kinda beyond that now."

"Why the secret, though?" Gillian wanted to know. "I'm on a scholarship myself."

"Yeah, but yours isn't to fill the minority quota. And you can afford to buy whatever you want," I pointed out.

"Nobody's laughing," Lissa said. "Why should they?"

"Vanessa would. And I thought Brett would. So that's why I kept it quiet all this time. Because I wanted them to see me as equal to them. Not—not as a fruit picker's grandkid."

"I don't think you have to worry about Brett," Shani said, eyebrows waggling. "That boy don't care whose grandkid you are."

"And besides, it totally fits," Lissa said. "If you hadn't gotten that job, you wouldn't have developed the pictures. And we probably wouldn't have known a thing until Mac disappeared and the school went up in smoke. So, see? That scholarship isn't anything to be ashamed of. It was all part of a bigger picture."

When you put it that way . . .

"So back to the story," Mac prompted me.

"Right. So, anyway, like I was saying, there was Brett, following me because of nothing more than a funny feeling in his gut. Both of us arrived just in time to help you—even though you told me you didn't think God would hear you. But He did. Because another five or ten minutes and we wouldn't even be having this conversation."

Mac burrowed down in her quilts, her brow furrowed. "I don't know about this big-picture idea. I still think it was a lot of guts and lucky timing." But to me, she sounded only eighty percent convinced.

Maybe the bigger picture didn't have anything to do with me. Maybe the Lord was trying to tell her something. Maybe it took people like Gillian and Lissa, who are totally not afraid to see God in the details, to bring it out into the open.

To give You the glory, Lord.

A lump formed in my throat as I thought about it. *Thank You. You gave Mac her life. I don't know what happened to David, but whatever that is, I know You'll help us get through it. Lord, I think You've put Your hand around Mac for good, whether she knows it or not. And maybe Brett, too.*

Gratitude welled up inside me, and love, and joy.

And then I remembered something else—something that took me from the big picture to the little corner that belonged to me.

Brett had asked me out for next Friday, and I hadn't given him a for-real answer.

I had no doubt how I'd answer him now.

chapter 21

THIS IS DREW ICHIKAWA reporting for Channel Four News, with an update on the story that broke late last night." An exterior shot of the main Spencer building appeared on the sixty-inch flat-screen TV in the Loyolas' dining room.

"Guys!" I waved the noise levels down so that everyone could hear. "This is it."

"New developments in the story of the Spencer Academy bomber have made this shocking case even more chilling. As we reported in our newscasts early this morning, David Brandon Nelson, the illegitimate half brother of Lady Lindsay MacPhail, a Scottish exchange student presently attending the elite Spencer Academy in Pacific Heights, had been stalking the young aristocrat for several weeks. It's not clear at this time what his motives were, as he has refused to talk to the police, but what is clear is that he made and then planted several bombs in various locations on the Spencer campus with the intent of detonating them when school began tomorrow. He then planned to use various weapons in his cache to massacre the students. His plot was foiled, however, by the quick thinking of a Spencer student who works at Piccadilly Photo, the photography shop where he took pictures of his handiwork to be developed."

Philip's face now filled the screen.

"Hey, that's my boss!" I exclaimed. This would be great exposure for the shop.

"The name of the student has not yet been released, and her whereabouts are at present unknown. With me is Philip Nolan, the owner of Piccadilly Photo. Philip, how does it feel to find out you have a hero working for you?"

"I've known she was unusual all along. Her family and her school should be proud," he had time to say before the shot switched back to Spencer, with crime-scene tape on the gates and cop cars in the front drive. Then it changed to a shot of the jail, where the reporter was standing.

"Nelson has been taken into custody, and this morning Channel Four News learned that he did indeed detonate a bomb at his own home at 1721 Bautista Court in the San Francisco State University area. Sources state that he had been holding Lady Lindsay against her will, but for reasons unclear to investigators at this time, she was not at the scene when the bomb went off.

"It is also not clear whether or not Nelson intended to take his own life. If so, he failed. Nelson's landlord, Thomas Henry Clyde, seventy-two, was caught in the blast and taken to the university hospital. We learned this morning that Mr. Clyde died of injuries he sustained as a result of the explosion."

I gasped and looked at Mac, then Brett, whose toast was suspended, uneaten, in front of his mouth as he watched the report.

"We'll give you developments on these tragic events as investigators work to find out exactly what happened. What is clear is that Nelson won't only be facing felony kidnapping and numerous charges of possessing a dangerous device with intent to injure persons or property. He'll now be charged with second-degree murder. This is Drew Ichikawa reporting for Channel Four News. Back to you, Randy."

The news switched to a story on a Middle Eastern prince who was coming to the States for an exchange term. Brett picked up the remote and muted the sound.

"That poor old man," Mac whispered. "I wonder if he ever knew David was making bombs in his attic."

"We'll never know." Did he have grandkids? Had they been watching the news? And how had he managed to be killed when David was obviously alive and well in some jail cell? I could only hope David had a beefy roommate whose name was Bubba.

The doorbell rang, and a couple minutes later, a flock of suits crowded into the dining room.

"Gentlemen," Mrs. Loyola greeted them. "Please. Join us for breakfast."

Sergeant Mason from last night spoke up. "Thanks, ma'am, but we're here to talk to the students. We can do that while they eat, if that's okay with everyone."

I wasn't sure what they intended to do if it wasn't okay, but anyway, they took us out one by one to take our statements. Mac got an extra guy—the one from the British Embassy, who looked as if he'd sat on a Popsicle stick but who she said turned out to be really nice. After, that is, he endured a supersized freakout from Mac about her being on some VIP list without anybody telling her. I could hear her yelling from where I sat next to Brett in the dining room. You had to feel sorry for the guy.

When it was my turn, I got Sergeant Mason himself. I told my story and only left out the part about The Kiss. That was between me and Brett. And, okay, my *chicas*, but that didn't count. Cops taking statements didn't need to know about it.

"So that was the reason they couldn't locate Lady Lindsay in the wreckage," he said, like he just wanted to be clear. "You cut her out of the duct tape with your nail scissors and she climbed out the back window, and both of you climbed down the side of the building and made your way through the backyard? Am I getting this right?"

I nodded, and when I looked up, he was gazing at me with an odd look on his face.

"That's why I called nine-one-one," I offered. "So people wouldn't worry. They'd know she was okay. The lady said she'd relayed the message. She did, didn't she?"

"Oh, yes, we got it. After the fire department nearly killed themselves trying to get to the area where we thought Her Lady-ship was being held."

"Mac hates when people call her that. Just so you know. I'm not in trouble, am I?" How ironic—to be arrested for *not* letting Mac's body be found in the wreckage.

"No. No, of course not." He still sounded a little shell-shocked. "I'm just amazed at this kind of courage. Miss Aragon, you are the bravest girl I've ever met."

I couldn't help it—I laughed. "Yeah, right. What else was I supposed to do? She's my friend."

"Your friend, indeed. With your permission, I'm going to rec-ommend that you be given a commendation."

Oh, now that really was funny. "Sure, whatever." It was nice of him to say it, though. "Hey, Sergeant? What's going to hap-pen to David? The news said he was charged with second-degree murder."

The policeman nodded. "He'll be held until his plea hearing, and then it will probably go to trial, considering the visibility and the seriousness of the case. I'm afraid you and Her—uh, Lady Lindsay will be required to testify. Is that going to be a problem?"

"Well, I've never actually met the guy."

"The jury will need to hear your version of events, though, as well as Brett Loyola's."

Deep inside, I did a happy dance. Even when all this was over, when he'd forgotten he'd asked me out and he'd gone back to not talking to anyone but the popular kids, we'd still see each other in court, standing shoulder-to-shoulder on the side of justice.

Sigh. How pathetic was that?

"Thanks for your help, Miss Aragon. And again, just let me repeat what others have said—your folks and your school should be proud of you."

He held the door of the little parlor for me and I walked out into the foyer, feeling one part relieved and two parts embarrassed. Ms. Curzon stood talking to the British Embassy guy, but Mac was nowhere in sight.

"Ah, Miss Aragon." She glanced at Sergeant Mason. "Is everything in order?"

"Yes, ma'am. I was just telling Miss Aragon that she is one courageous young lady. Spencer Academy should be proud."

She smiled, but there was something absent in it. As though she were putting it on like a new paint job, but there was still engine trouble underneath.

Listen to me with the car metaphors. One night riding with Brett in his Camaro and I was an expert.

"If you need nothing else, I'd like to speak to her."

He made a be-my-guest gesture toward the parlor and I followed her in. "Ma'am?"

"Sit down, Miss Aragon."

I sat in the same chair I'd just used, only now I scrooched all the way to the edge of it.

"I understand we owe you a great debt. Without you and Brett, the news reports might have been quite different, and the phone calls I made to Scotland and London this morning might not have had the same happy result."

"Thank you, ma'am. I mean, you're welcome."

"Which puts me in a very difficult position."

"It does?" She'd said herself that the results had been happy.

"You see, delighted though I am that Lady Lindsay is safe and you and Brett emerged from this ordeal unscathed, the fact remains that the entire series of events happened because you disobeyed a direct request from me."

It took me a second to figure this out.

Oh. In the taxi. When she'd told me to be back in my room at school in ten minutes, and I'd told the cabbie to take me to Bautista Court instead.

So I'd hit "override" in her little script. But we'd saved Mac. We were all okay. How was this a problem?

I guess she must have seen the question in my face, because she said, "You must know that several students heard me ask you to come back. How am I to maintain order among them if it's known that people can disobey me and get away with it?"

"But I didn't disobey. Well, okay, I did, but only because the situation was urgent. We saved Mac's life, ma'am. Surely that balances out my not doing what you said."

"In the cosmic scheme of things, no doubt it does. But without you in the picture, the police would still have arrived. Maybe Lady Lindsay could still have been saved, or she would have found her way to safety herself. However, in the Spencer Academy scheme of things, I am still headmistress and you are still a student."

I eyed her, a feeling of dread beginning to poke at my stomach.

"Miss Aragon, I'm very sorry to say that I'm going to have to suspend you from school."

MY FATHER COMPLETELY lost it and canceled his trip to Singapore.

I got deported down to San Jose for my five-day sentence and then had the fun job of explaining to him that this little embarrassment was just to save Ms. Curzon's pride and her rep with the students. It didn't really have anything to do with me or what had happened to Mac.

He didn't buy it.

In fact, I came about two inches from being enrolled at a public school in the South Bay. The only thing that saved me was the fact that there was only a month of my junior year left and they wouldn't take me.

He confiscated my phone as further punishment and went back to work, leaving me with the condo to myself from eight until four, when Antony got home from school.

There was nothing to do except watch the news. Oh, and do schoolwork. At least Papa hadn't cut off computer privileges, which meant I still had e-mail and IM to keep myself connected to the real world.

If you want the truth, it felt eerily like last term. Being accused of stuff other people did was getting really old.

LMansfield	We miss you!
CAragon	Not as much as I miss you guys.
LMansfield	Only 3 days left to go. Can you come back for the weekend?
CAragon	I don't know. Probably not. Papa is super-upset. Maybe I should have him talk to Sgt. Mason. At least he thinks I did something right.
LMansfield	He's not the only one. I take it you didn't hear?
CAragon	??
LMansfield	Check out next week's *People*. On newsstands everywhere Monday.
CAragon	Tell this second, or I'll sic Shani on you!
LMansfield	Mac gave a big interview. There's going to be a 4-page feature and pix of all of us.

CAragon	!!!
LMansfield	VT is crazed. Wait till you see the quote from Brett.
CAragon	OMG. What did he say?
LMansfield	Not telling. It's a surprise to welcome you back.
CAragon	Lissa! Argghhhh!

On Wednesday, my least favorite day of the week, naturally my mother called.

"*Mi'ja*, I'm so glad to hear your voice. After your father called, I've been following the news reports on sfgate-dot-com. What an ordeal you've been through!"

"Hi, Mama. When did he call you?"

"Sunday, before we left for church."

And she'd waited until *Wednesday* to talk to me?

"Honestly, Carly, while it was terribly brave, don't you think you should have done what your headmistress asked? Your father says you've been suspended."

"Yes. It's just a formality."

"A formality that will go on your transcript. Carolina, you have to learn to think things through before you go diving headlong into them."

"There wasn't time." My throat felt tight. And my lips weren't forming words very well. "We did save my friend's life."

"Yes, Lady Lindsay somebody, right? First the daughter of the Italian princess, now an earl's daughter. Soon you'll be too good for your own family."

"Thanks for calling, Mama. I have tons of homework to do, so I'd better go. They e-mail it to me by the pound, it feels like."

"One thing, darling. Have you given any more thought to being my bridesmaid?"

This was so like my mother. I'd just been through a huge crisis, and all she could think about was herself. "No, Mama. I've been kind of busy."

"Please do think about it. We've settled on a date—December. A Christmas wedding in Santa Fe. So that only leaves seven months to plan."

"You'll have to plan without me, then. I'll probably be in Santa Barbara."

"Carolina." She sounded like she was about to cry.

My computer beeped, announcing the arrival of an e-mail message. "I have to go, Mama. I think more homework just arrived."

To my amazement, she didn't argue. "Good-bye, darling. *Te amo*."

"I love you, too." Though I had to work pretty hard to remember what that felt like.

ON THURSDAY a letter came via FedEx. As I signed for it, I figured it was probably an official communiqué from Spencer, telling me not to come back next year or something equally horrible. I let it sit on the counter for about twenty minutes before curiosity got the best of me.

Dear Miss Aragon,

On behalf of the City of San Francisco and the Board of Supervisors, I would like to take this opportunity to thank you for your part in averting what could have been one of the worst tragedies in this city's history. Your bravery and quick thinking were instrumental in saving the life not only of a fellow student but of countless others at Spencer Academy.

Our city is grateful to you. To show our appreciation, and by recommendation of the San Francisco Police Department and a resolution of the San Francisco Board of Supervisors, I would like to invite you to a ceremony on the steps of City Hall, where I will present you with a commendation, the highest honor it is in my power to bestow.

Please join us at two o'clock on Saturday, June 6, and invite as many of your family and friends as you would like. I look forward to conveying my thanks to you personally.

With gratitude,

Gavin Newsom

Mayor

TEXT MESSAGE

Brett Loyola	Hey girl, it's Friday . . . 6:00 p.m. to be exact.
Carolina Aragon	Hi.
Brett Loyola	So what would you like to do?
Carolina Aragon	??
Brett Loyola	You said you'd see a movie with me or something. Re-member? Last week, in all the bizarrity?
Carolina Aragon	Is that a word?
Brett Loyola	It is now.
Carolina Aragon	I thought you were kidding.
Brett Loyola	No. Uh . . . did I make a mistake?
Carolina Aragon	No, no! But I'm kinda far away. Still in San Jose.
Brett Loyola	S'okay. I am too.
Carolina Aragon	Where?
Brett Loyola	On your doorstep, texting from my iPhone.
Brett Loyola	Surprise!

chapter 22

I SWEAR, MY FEET didn't even touch the stairs as I flew down them. This must be a joke. But on the off chance it wasn't, frantic hope fluttered inside me like a trapped bird. I wrenched the front door open and let out a squeak that was half surprise, half-disbelieving laugh.

"Hey." Brett pocketed his iPhone and grinned at me. "I hope this is okay. Just showing up, I mean."

"It's totally okay," I said, practically gasping. *Calm down. Breathe. Kick in, hostess reflex.* "Come on in. Have you had supper yet?"

"I was thinking I could talk you into going somewhere to eat before we caught that movie."

"Carolina, who is this?"

I turned as my father came out of the dining room, which he used as his office. Up on the stairs, Antony peered through the railing. "Carly's got a boyfriend. Carly's got a boyfriend," he sang in his raspy, off-key voice.

Brat. Color rose in my face like a hot wave.

"Antony, where are your manners?" Papa demanded. "Come down and behave."

"Mr. Aragon, it's nice to meet you, sir." Brett shook my father's hand. "I'm Brett Loyola. The one who shared Carly's, um, experience recently."

"Brett Loyola. Ah. As in Loyola Investment Corporation?"

"Guilty."

"Not that that matters. I'm very happy to meet the young man who helped my daughter so much. I think the two of you make a very impressive team." Papa took Antony by the shoulders. "This is my son, Antony."

"Hi, Brett," he chirped, all nearly-thirteen cool. "You're the one with the '68 Camaro, right?"

"That's right. It's parked outside. Maybe—if it's okay with your dad—we can go for a ride later."

"Cool!" Antony twisted out of Papa's grip and scampered back upstairs to his video game.

The warm, spicy smell of a *chile verde* casserole permeated the condo. "I hope you'll stay for dinner, Brett," Papa said. "Carly spent half the afternoon putting it together—it would be a shame to waste it."

"You can cook?" Brett looked at me. "On top of everything else?"

Everything else? "Sure. I've been cooking since"—*my mother left us*— "for a couple of years now. Please stay." I moved into the big open kitchen, and both he and Papa followed. I smothered a smile as Brett's nostrils dilated. He must be starving. "And about the movie . . ."

"Movie?" Papa frowned at me. "What is this? You're grounded, remember?"

How could I forget? "You didn't say anything about having friends over." Mostly because all my friends were in San Francisco now. And I ignored the fact that, up until this point, I'd kept them away because I'd been ashamed of how we lived. No big house, no BMW in the garage, no acreage manicured by a Mexican gardener who sent most of his paycheck across the border to feed his family.

But here was Brett, in our suburban condo, dragging in deep breaths of pork-and-Hatch-chile-scented air and looking as if all he wanted was to get comfortable with a big plate of it right this moment. I doubt he'd even noticed that there weren't any Italian silk drapes within ten miles.

My father's lips twitched. "You're right. I didn't. I hope Brett doesn't mind if you take a rain check on that movie."

"Actually, I'm thinking it would be kinda cool to see *Crossing Blades* again." Brett looked at me. "Leaving out the fact that you're buds with the director's daughter, I heard you like historical stuff."

Okay, we were moving back into the Twilight Zone. "I have it here." Had he really said *Crossing Blades*? My all-time favorite movie? I knew practically every line, but watching it with Brett would make it a new experience.

"But the extended-version DVD just came out. Do you have that?"

"No way." Being grounded meant no fast trips to Circuit City to get the new releases.

"I had a little talk with your friend Shani and she told me. So I picked it up the other day when I was getting some cables."

"You like period movies?" The captain of the rowing team, one of the most popular guys in school? It was like worlds colliding.

"Sure. *Crossing Blades*, *Pirates*, *Hornblower*, *Sharpe's Rifles*, you name it. I draw the line at *Forsyte* and *Bleak House*, even if that girl who plays Ada is hot."

I laughed. "If you know that, you must have watched them." Military strategy and wonderful dresses. Clearly we were made for each other. It was a sign.

The oven timer pinged. I tore myself away from him and got the plates down out of the cupboard. "Dinner's ready. Papa, can you unplug Antony from his game and tell him to wash his hands?"

I threw together a salad, set out chips and my latest experiment with red chile salsa, and ten minutes later I was sitting next to Brett Loyola eating casserole. Worlds had collided. And he didn't seem to mind at all.

After a meal during which Papa grilled Brett on everything from his GPA to his golf handicap, my father obligingly disappeared. Naturally, Antony did the same before I could rope him into loading the dishwasher. Instead, Brett started putting wet plates into it.

"You don't have to do that," I said. "Please. I feel weird about it."

"Why? My mom would kill me if she thought I was sitting around on my butt, watching someone else work."

"She would?"

"Sure. You saw her. She runs a tight ship."

She gave out hugs, too. "Tell her thank you again for letting all of us be quarantined at your place. It was way more fun than going to the Four Seasons."

He closed the dishwasher door while I finished wiping down the counters. "That's what I thought when I asked her to lean on Curzon and invite you."

I draped the washcloth over the faucet. "Why did you do that? Not that I'm not happy you did. But it's not like we were all best buds with you."

"Is that what you think? Even after that night?"

I could fall into his eyes. Fall and fall and never come up again. That dark-chocolate gaze forced me to peel away all the layers of self-consciousness and mistaken impressions that I'd put up.

"I don't know what to think."

The mayor thought I had courage. But what Brett and I had

done wasn't courageous—we just did what had to be done to make sure our friend was safe. Opening my mouth and speaking now took the real thing.

"I want to think you like me the way I like you," I said slowly. "But I'm afraid that we're both just reacting to all the danger. Like we shared this amazing experience, but in real life we'll just go back to being the way we were."

He gazed at me and I wondered if I'd gone too far. Made too many assumptions. Put into words what didn't exist, and now it would disappear.

"Is that what you want?" he asked me. "To go back to the way we were?"

"No," I whispered. "I want us to be friends."

"Just friends?"

I had nothing left to lose. He could laugh at me if he wanted, but I was going to say this even if it cost me his friendship—and more.

"No. I want to hang out with you after school and watch *Crossing Blades* another six million times and take you and your noisy car over to show my Tío Miguel. I want to go out somewhere special with you, wearing the dress I'm going to make for Design Your Dreams. And I want to know what you said to *People* magazine about me, because it's driving me crazy."

It all came out in a rush, and I didn't know whether to look at him or not.

And then he laughed. One of those great big laughs that makes you laugh, too. And before I could ask myself what it meant, he closed the distance between us and slid his arms around me.

My eyes came almost level with his chin, which meant I had to tip my head back to look him in the face.

"You really want to know?"

"Everything. All of it," I said softly.

"I don't know what they'll print, but I told the reporter that

that night was the scariest night of my life. Not because of bombs or crazy guys or houses blowing up, but because I totally lost it and kissed this girl."

"You told a reporter you kissed me?" Ohmigosh. People all over the country were going to *read* this!

"I told her I'd never met a braver person than Carly Aragon, and I was feeling like a weenie because I hadn't got up the guts to ask her to this big school event in June."

"You did? I mean, you were?"

"Yes."

"Then how come when we went to that party, you danced with Mac and not me?"

His lashes dipped, and then our gazes reconnected. "Because it was easier. I thought I could work up the nerve if I started with your friend. Except Cal and every other guy in the room got there ahead of me."

I lifted my chin. "Serves you right. I felt like the consolation prize when we finally got together."

"I knew something was off." His gaze turned penitent. "I was stupid and a chicken and I got what I deserved. But nobody's getting in the way now. So. Carly. Will you let me escort you to the big DYD reception, and then go with me to the after-party?"

My poor dress. Its beautiful Worth detailing was still in muslin, gathering dust on my abandoned dress form in San Francisco. "I don't even have any fabric yet," I blurted, and if I hadn't had my arms looped around his waist, I'd have clonked myself on the forehead for being so stupid. "I mean, yes. Yes, I'd love to go with you."

"Fabric. Please don't tell me you're like my mom. She has a whole room full of fabric that she gets from her friends in Italy. If you want, I can talk to her about your using some of it." His eyes were warm, but on my back, I felt a tremor in his hands.

Wow. Brett Loyola was *nervous*. As if this was super-personal but he wanted me and his mom to connect anyway. I'd *walk* to San Francisco and beg his mother on my knees if it meant looking at a roomful of Italian fabrics.

"But in the meantime," he said, "since nothing is about to explode except maybe your dad, and we're alone, can I ask you something?"

I nodded, my whole being fixated on his next words.

"Can—can I kiss you again?"

Now *that's* what I call courage.

And in case you're wondering, I said yes.

about the author

Shelley Adina wrote her first teen novel when she was thirteen. It was rejected by the literary publisher to whom she sent it, but he did say she knew how to tell a story. That was enough to keep her going through the rest of her adolescence, a career, a move to another country, a B.A. in Literature, an M.A. in Writing Popular Fiction, and countless manuscript pages.

Shelley is a world traveler and pop culture junkie with an incurable addiction to designer handbags. She knows the value of a relationship with a gracious God and loving Christian friends and loves writing about fun and faith—with a side of glamour. Between books, Shelley loves traveling, listening to and making music, and watching all kinds of movies.

IF YOU LIKED

be strong & curvaceous,

you'll love the fourth book in the series:

who made you a princess?

available in May 2009!

Turn the page for a sneak peek . . .

And when he went out the second day, behold, two men of the Hebrews strove together: and he said to him that did the wrong, Wherefore smitest thou thy fellow? And he said, Who made thee a prince and a judge over us?
—*Exodus 2:13-14 (KJV)*

Choose my instruction instead of silver, knowledge rather than choice gold, for wisdom is more precious than rubies, and nothing you desire can compare with her.
—*Proverbs 8:10-11 (NIV)*

chapter 1

NOTHING SAYS "ALONE" like a wide, sandy beach on the western edge of the continent, with the sun going down in a smear of red and orange. Girlfriends, I am the go-to girl for alone. Or at least, that's what I used to think. Not anymore, though, because nothing says "alive" like a fire snapping and hissing at your feet, and half a dozen of your BFFs laughing and talking around you.

Like the T-shirt says, life is good.

My name's Shani Amira Marjorie Hanna, and up until I started going to Spencer Academy in my freshman year, all I wanted to do was get in, scoop as many A's as I could, and get out. College, yeah. Adulthood. Being the boss of me. Social life? Who cared? I'd treat it the way I'd done in middle school, making my own way and watching people brush by me, all disappearing into good-bye like they were flowing down a river.

Then when I was a junior, I met the girls, and things started to change whether I wanted them to or not. Or maybe it was just me. Doing the changing, I mean.

Now we were all seniors and I was beginning to see that all this "I am an island" stuff was just a bunch of smoke. Cuz I was not an island, like the Catalinas sitting out there on the hazy horizon. Not even a peninsula. I was so done with all that.

Lissa Mansfield sat on the other side of the fire from me while this adorable Jared Padalecki lookalike named Kaz Griffin sat next to her trying to act like the best friend she thought he was. Lissa needs a smack upside the head, if you want my opinion. Either that or someone needs to make a serious play for him to wake her up. But it's not going to be me. I've got cuter fish to fry. Heh. More about that later.

"I can't believe this is the last weekend of summer vacation," Carly moaned for about the fifth time since Kaz lit the fire and we all got comfortable in the sand around it. "It's gone so fast."

"That's because you've only been here a week." I handed her the bag of tortilla chips. "What about me? I've been here for a month and I still can't believe we have to go up to San Francisco on Tuesday."

"I'm so jealous." Carly bumped me with her shoulder and dipped a handful of chips in a big plastic container of salsa she'd made this morning with fresh tomatoes and cilantro and little bits of—get this—cantaloupe. She made one the other day with carrots in it. I don't know how she comes up with this stuff, but it's all good. We had a cooler full of food to munch on. No burnt weenies for this crowd. Uh-uh. What we can't order delivered, Carly can make. "A whole month at Casa Mansfield with your own private beach and everything."

"And to think I could have gone back to Chicago and spent the whole summer throwing parties and trashing the McMansion." I sighed with regret. "Instead, I had to put up with a month in the

Hamptons with the Changs and then a month out here fighting Lissa for her bathroom."

"Hey, you could have used one of the other ones," Lissa protested, trying to keep Kaz from snagging the rest of her turkey, avocado, and alfalfa sprouts sandwich.

I grinned at her. Who wanted to walk down the hot sandstone patio to one of the other bathrooms when she, Carly, and I had this beautiful Spanish terrazzo-looking wing of the house to ourselves? Carly and I were in her sister's old room, which looked out on this garden with a fountain and big ferns and grasses and flowering trees. And beyond that was the ocean. It was the kind of place you didn't want to leave, even to go to the bathroom.

I contrasted it with the freezing wind off Lake Michigan in the winter and the long empty hallways of the McMansion, where I always felt like a guest. You know—like you're welcome but the hosts don't really know what to do with you. I mean, my mom has told me point blank, with a kind of embarrassed little laugh, that she can't imagine what happened. The Pill and her careful preventive measures couldn't all have failed on the same night.

Organic waste happens. Whatever.

The point is, I arrived seventeen years ago and they had to adjust. I think they love me. My dad always reads my report cards, and he used to take me to blues clubs to listen to the musicians doing sound checks before the doors opened. That was before my mom found out. Then I had to wait until I was twelve and we went to the early shows, which were never as good as the late ones I snuck into whenever my parents went on one of their trips.

They travel a lot. Dad owns this massive petroleum exploration company, and Mom's been everywhere from Alaska to New Zealand. I saw a lot of great shows with whichever member of the staff I could bribe to take me and swear I was sixteen. Albert

King, B.B. King, Buddy Guy, Roomful of Blues—I saw them all.

A G-minor chord rippled out over the crackle of the fire, and I smiled a slow smile. My second favorite sound in the world (right after the sound of M&Ms pouring into a dish). On my left, Danyel had pulled out his guitar and tuned it while I was lost in la-la land, listening to the waves come in.

Lissa says there are some things you just know. And somehow, I just knew that I was going to be more to Danyel Johnstone than just a friend of his friend Kaz's friend Lissa, if you hear what I'm saying. I was done with being alone, but that didn't mean I couldn't stand out from the crowd.

Don't get me wrong, I really like this crowd. Carly especially— she's like the sister I would have designed for myself. And Lissa, too, though sometimes I wonder if she can be real. I mean, how can you be blond and tall and rich and wear clothes the way she does and still be so nice? There has to be a flaw in there some- where, but if she's got any, she keeps them under wraps.

Gillian, who we'd see in a couple of days, has really grown on me. I couldn't stand her at first—she's one of those people you notice. I only hung around her because Carly liked her. But somewhere between her going out with this loser brain trust and then her hooking up with Jeremy Clay, who's a friend of mine, I got to know her. And staying with her family last Christmas, which could have been massively awkward, was actually fun. The last month in the Hamptons with them was a total blast. The only good thing about leaving was knowing I was going to see the rest of the crew here in Santa Barbara.

The one person I still wasn't sure about was Mac, aka Lady Lindsay MacPhail, who did an exchange term at school in the spring. Getting to know her is like besieging a castle—which is totally appropriate considering she *lives* in one. She and Carly are tight, and we all e-mailed and IM-ed like fiends all summer, but I'm still not sure. I mean, she has a lot to deal with right now with her family and everything. And the likelihood of us seeing each other again is kind of low, so maybe I don't have to make up my mind about her. Maybe I'll just let her go the way I let the kids in middle school go.

Danyel began to get serious about bending his notes instead of finger picking, and I knew he was about to sing. Oh, man, could the night get any more perfect? Even though we'd probably burn the handmade marshmallows from Williams Sonoma, tonight was still the best time I'd ever had.

The only thing that would make it perfect would be finding some way to be alone together. I hadn't been here more than a day when Danyel and Kaz had come loping down the beach. I'd taken one look at those eyes and those cut cheekbones and, okay, a very fine set of abs, and decided here was someone I wanted to know a whole lot better. And I did, now, after a couple of weeks. But soon we'd go off to S.F. and he and Kaz would go back to Pacific High. When we pulled out in Gabe Mansfield's SUV, I wanted there to be something more between us than an air kiss and a handshake, you know what I mean?

I wanted something to be *settled*. Neither of us had talked about it, but both of us knew it was there. Unspoken longing is all very well in poetry, but I'm the outspoken type. I like things out there where I can touch them.

In a manner of speaking.

Danyel sat between Kaz and me, cross-legged and bare-chested, looking as comfortable in his surf jams as if he lived in them. Come to think of it, he *did* live in them. His, Kaz's, and Lissa's boards were stuck in the sand behind us. They'd spent most of the afternoon out there on the waves. I tried to keep from ogling his pecs. Not that I didn't appreciate the view, because trust me, it was fine, but I know a man wants to be appreciated for his talents and his mind.

Of course, he could ogle me anytime he wanted. Maybe he had but was too much of a gentleman to let me see it.

Danyel's melody sounded familiar—something Gillian played before her prayer circles at school got started. I nudged Carly. "You guys going to church tomorrow?"

She nodded and lifted her chin at Lissa to get her attention. "We are, right?"

"Wouldn't miss it," Lissa said. "Kaz and his family, too. Last chance of the summer to all go together."

And where Kaz went, Danyel went. Happy thought. Certainly made church interesting for me.

"Why, are you thinking of coming?" Carly's brows rose a little, and I heard the question she wasn't asking. *What brought this on?*

It's not like I'm anti-religion or anything. I just don't know that much about it. My parents don't go to church, so I didn't catch the habit from them. When she was alive and I was a little girl, my grandma used to take me to the one in her neighborhood across town. I thought it was an adventure, riding the bus instead of being driven in the BMW. And the gospel choir was like nothing I'd ever seen, all waving their arms in the air and singing to raise the roof. I always thought they were trying to deafen God if they could just get up enough volume.

So I like the music part. I'm just not sure about the God part.

"Yeah, I was." I gave her a look. "You got a problem with that?"

"Not me. You haven't exactly been beating Lissa to the car on Sundays, that's all. From what I hear."

"That's because we walk, smart apple."

"Uh-huh." She sat back on her hands, an "I *so* see right through you" smile turning up the corners of her mouth. "I bet." That smile told me she knew exactly what my motivation was. And it wasn't to keep the pew warm.

The music changed and Danyel's voice lifted into a lonely blues melody, pouring over my half-joking words like cream. I just melted right there on the spot. Man, could that boy sing.

Blue water, blue sky
Blue day, girl, do you think that I
Don't see you, yeah I do.
Long sunset, long road,
Long life, girl, but I think you know
What I need, yeah, you do.

I do a little singing myself, so I know talent when I hear it. And I'd have bet you that month's allowance that Danyel had composed that one himself. He segued into the chorus and then the bridge, its rhythms straight out of Mississippi but the tune something new, something that fit the sadness and the hope of the words.

Wait a minute.

Blue day? Long sunset? Long road? As in, a long road to San Francisco?

Whoa. Could Danyel be trying to tell someone something? "You think that I don't see you"? Well, if that didn't describe *me*, I didn't know what would. Ohmigosh.

Could he be trying to tell me his feelings with a song? Musicians were like that. They couldn't tell a person something to her face, or they were too shy, or it was just too hard to get out, so they poured it into their music. For them, maybe it was easier to perform something than to get personal with it.

Oh, man.

Be cool, girl. Let him finish. Then find a way to tell him you understand—and you want it, too.

The last of the notes blew away on the breeze, and a big comber smashed itself on the sand, making a sound like a kettledrum to finish it off. I clapped, and the others joined in.

"Did you write that yourself?" Lissa removed a marshmallow from her stick and passed it to him. "It was great."

Danyel shrugged one shoulder. "Tune's been bugging me for a while and the words just came to me. You know, like an IM or something."

Carly laughed, and Kaz's forehead wrinkled for a second in a frown before he did, too.

I love modesty in a man. With that kind of talent, you couldn't blame Danyel for thinking he was all that.

Should I say something? The breath backed up in my chest. *Say it. You'll lose the moment.* "So who's it about?" I blurted, then felt myself blush.

"Can't tell." His head was bent as he picked a handful of notes and turned them into a little melody. "Some girl, probably."

"Some girl who's leaving?" I said, trying for a teasing tone. "Is that a good-bye?"

"Could be."

I wished I had the guts to come out and ask if he'd written the song for me—for us—but I just couldn't. Not with everyone sitting there. With one look at Carly, whose eyes held a distinct "What's up with you?" expression, I lost my nerve and shut up. Which, as any of the girls could tell you, doesn't happen very often.

Danyel launched into another song—some praise thing that everyone knew but me. And then another, and then a cheesy old John Denver number that at least I knew the words to, and then a bunch of goofy songs half of us had learned at camp when we were kids. And then it was nearly midnight and Kaz got up and stretched.

He's a tall guy. He stretches a long way. "I'm running the mixer for the early service tomorrow, so I've got to go."

Danyel got up and I just stopped myself from saying, "No, not yet." Instead, I watched him sling the guitar over one shoulder and yank his board out of the sand. "Are you going to early service, too?" I asked him.

"Yeah," he said, sounding a little surprised. "I'm in the band, remember?"

Argh! As if I didn't know. As if I hadn't sat there three Sundays in a row, watching his hands move on the frets and the light make shadows under his cheekbones.

"I just meant—I see you at the late one when we go. I didn't know you went to both." Stutter, bumble. *Oh, just stop talking, girl. You've been perfectly comfortable talking to him so far. What's the matter?*

"I don't, usually. But tomorrow they're doing full band at early service, too. Last one before all the *touristas* go home. Next week we'll be back to normal." He smiled at me. "See you then."

Was he looking forward to seeing me, or was he just being nice? "I hope so," I managed.

"Kaz, you coming?"

Kaz bent to the fire and ran a stick through the coals, separating them. "Just let me put this out. Lissa, where's the bucket?"

"Here." While I'd been obsessing over Danyel, Lissa had run down to the waterline and filled a gallon pail. You could tell they'd done this about a million times. She poured the water on the fire and it blew a cloud of steam into the air. The orange coals gave it up with a hiss.

I looked up to say something to Danyel about it and saw that he was already fifty feet away, board under his arm like it weighed nothing, heading down the beach to the public lot where he usually parked his Jeep.

I stared down into the coals, wet and dying.

I couldn't let the night go out like this.

"Danyel, wait!" The sand polished the soles of my bare feet better than the pumice bar at my pedicurist's as I ran to catch up with him. A fast glance behind me told me Lissa had stepped up and begun talking to Kaz, giving me a few seconds alone.

I owed her, big-time.

"What's up, ma?" He planted the board and set the guitar case down. "Forget something?"

"Yes," I blurted. "I forgot to tell you that I think you're amazing."

He blinked. "Whoa." The barest hint of a smile tickled the corners of his lips.

I might not get another chance as good as this one. I rushed on before I lost my nerve. "I know there's something going on here and we're all leaving on Tuesday and I need to know if you—if you feel the same way."

"About . . . ?"

"About me. As I feel about you."

He put both hands on his hips and gazed down at the sand. "Oh."

Cold engulfed me, as if I'd just plunged face-first into the dark waves twenty feet away. "Oh," I echoed. "Never mind. I guess I got it wrong." I stepped back. "Forget about it. No harm done."

"No, Shani, wait—"

But I didn't want to hear the "we can still be friends" speech. I didn't want to hear anything except the wind in my ears as I ran away.

Delivered by Hand
September 21, 2009

His Serene Highness Sheikh Amir al-Aarez
Kingdom of Yasir
Office of the Private Secretary

Dr. Natalie Curzon, Principal
Spencer Academy
2600 Washington Street
San Francisco, California 94111

Dr. Curzon, greetings.

I am pleased to inform you that final security checks of the Spencer Academy campus have been completed. As outlined by our office earlier this summer, this letter will confirm His Serene Highness's requirements for the accommodation of his beloved son, Prince Rashid al Amir.

1. It is not acceptable that the heir to the Lion Throne should stay in anything other than a private room. Therefore, Mr. Travis Fanshaw must be removed to another room.
2. In view of the regrettable incident involving Lady Lindsay MacPhail of the United Kingdom last May, the Prince's personal security force will number not one agent, but two. One agent will be accommodated within the Prince's room itself. The other will sleep in an adjoining room. I trust the students will appreciate the privilege of supporting the safety of the heir and will not be too greatly discommoded.
3. If the Prince prefers not to take his lessons with the other students, male tutors will be provided for him.
4. The Prince will not under any circumstances disrobe in the presence of others. Therefore his participation in physical education classes will be limited to those that do not require a uniform or special clothing. Should it be his wish to participate, he will require private shower and toilet facilities.
5. The Prince's focus shall be on his studies. Please do your utmost to encourage him in academic endeavors, keeping always in mind that you are assisting in the education of a future king.

I am sure that Spencer Academy, its faculty, and its students are cognizant of the honor done their institution. I trust His Highness will enjoy a happy and productive term.

With very best wishes for your health, I remain,

Farshad Ma'mun

Farshad Ma'mun, MBA, Ph.D.
Private Secretary to His Serene Highness
The Sheikh of Yasir

If you enjoyed

be strong & curvaceous

check out the book that started it all:

it's all about us

Tall, blonde Lissa Mansfield is used to being one of the "in" crowd, but being accepted by the popular girls at posh Spencer Academy boarding school in San Francisco is turning out to be harder than she thought. And then there's her New-York-loudmouth roommate, Gillian Chang, who's not just happy to be a Christian herself—she's determined to out Lissa, too! If Lissa can just keep her faith under wraps long enough to hook Callum McCloud, the hottest guy in school, she'll be golden.

But when Callum pressures her to go all the way with him, Lissa has to decide for herself how far is too far. How can she see that line when he's so gorgeous and popular and she's so dazzled? And besides, she's too busy shopping for a Valentino and booking the hottest celeb for the Benefactors' Ball. Who knew finding a place at Spencer Academy would be so complicated?

Available at bookstores now!